Praise for the Author

"Goss's greatest strengths, which are significant and not easily mastered, are authentic dialogue and solid plotting." —BlueInk Review

"Her [Goss] manner of developing her plots and her characters is sure, polished, and yet with enough co-existing suspense to hold our attention to the last page." —San Francisco Review of Books

"This author [Goss] does a fantastic job at creating realistic characters..." —Portsmouth Review

"Author Inge-Lise Goss has developed an engaging and intriguing mystery in Diamonds and Lies." —Readers' Favorite Reviewer

Diamonds and Lies

Inge-Lise Goss

Olivebranch Press

Acknowledgments

My gratitude goes out to my outstanding editors, Jeff LaFerney and Nancy Buford. Their suggestions, comments, and edits greatly enhanced my story. I also want to extend a special thanks to C. Michelle McCarty for generously giving her time to help me polish my story. Last, but not least, I'd like to thank Ashley Fontainne for designing such a wonderful cover.

Prologue

Two days after his last heist, the police surrounded Leo Carlyle's house. A bag holding stolen rare coins sat on his table, ready for delivery to the buyer. When the doorbell rang, Carlyle realized he couldn't escape. Even though there had been a problem with that job, he had made sure not to leave a trail. Wondering how the police managed to track him, he surrendered without incident.

During the heist, Carlyle knew he had screwed up when a shot was fired by the third security guard, a man he hadn't taken into consideration in the planning stage. Andy and Mia, his accomplices and children, had flawlessly followed through with their designated tasks. Andy had cracked the safe and removed the irreplaceable coins. Mia, in addition to helping Andy disable the alarm system, had kept the guard at the main entrance busy. It was their father, the one in charge, who had messed up.

Carlyle thought the job would be easy—in and out

within ten minutes. It was minute eleven when the first shot was fired. Andy had reached the van. Mia was a short distance behind him. In order to keep the main guard busy, she wore a seductive disguise, an easy target. Had it not been for Andy's swift action, pulling Mia to the ground, she would've been shot. Gripping her arm, Andy dragged her to the getaway vehicle. At that moment, Carlyle was pleased that his son had remembered what he had said: "Never come back for me. I'll be okay."

The prosecutor had all the evidence needed to convict Carlyle but nothing that would lead the cops to Andy and Mia. Despite Carlyle's refusal to name his accomplices, in exchange for pleading guilty, his attorney plea bargained. Carlyle was sentenced to twenty years and would be up for parole in fifteen.

He had only been in prison a week when he received an unexpected and unwanted visitor. "You could've gotten her killed," said the attorney for a man he feared. "Remember the agreement?"

"Come on. I'm locked up. Can't make it right."

"And you were paid fifty percent in advance for those coins. Where's the money?"

"It was in my house. The police confiscated it."

The attorney scoffed. "I will verify your claim."

Less than a month later, Leo Carlyle was found with a shiv in his neck. He'd bled to death in his cell.

Chapter 1

Mia Sloan checked her watch, trepidation mounting as if she were checking a bomb's timepiece while trying to defuse the explosive device. Andy's call had awakened her early, wanting to meet for breakfast with his favorite sister. As his only sibling, Mia knew his *modus operandi* when he needed her help. But these days, meetings with Andy had to be quick. As an account executive at a large advertising agency, her responsibilities were increasing. Mia valued her career but could never ignore her brother's needs.

Walking toward the diner on the Upper West Side of New York City, Mia both dreaded and looked forward to seeing her brother. When their mother died, their father entered their lives again. After not being around for sixteen years—ever since Mia was born—Leo Carlyle took over every aspect of their lives. Before he was killed in prison, he had groomed his children to become skilled burglars. Andy located the targets with help from his father's network while Mia, three years younger, set up the mark. Her sophisticated touch with unsuspecting, wealthy men never failed. She distracted the mark while Andy, a skilled safecracker, did the heist. Occasionally, she assisted in the actual theft.

Mia arrived at Andy's favorite haunt, went straight to the diner's back booth, and threw her arms around her brother, giving him a big hug.

"Hi, Sis. I ordered us both the slam dunk breakfast."

"Andy, you know I can't eat that much."

"That's what I like to hear. I'll have no problem finishing off what's left on your plate."

Their orders barely landed before Andy began flirting with the cute, petite waitress.

"How's Maxine?" Mia interrupted her brother to ask about his new squeeze. Andy went through girlfriends faster than he did money. Women seemed drawn to his masculine body, accentuated nicely with black, wavy hair, dark eyes, and a bronze complexion. Andy's dark features sometimes made Mia wonder if they had the same dad since she was fair with light brown hair and blue eyes, the opposite of her brother, dad, and mom.

"Great."

Mia's eyebrows rose. *I bet.* "How's the body shop?"

Andy had bought an auto repair shop two years earlier after a big job. Restoring and fixing racing cars, his passion, let him take the occasional spin around a track. Speed and danger attracted him.

"No complaints," Andy said between bites. "Business is increasing, so I hired another mechanic."

As they ate in silence, Mia's stomach churned. Andy hadn't insisted on seeing her before she went to work just to have breakfast with her. She wished he would blurt out the reason, but that wasn't his style. He always waited to the last minute before he dropped the axe. "I have to take off. I have to prepare for a ten o'clock meeting."

Andy eyed her plate, "But you're not through eating."

Mia patted her napkin over her lips and placed it next to her plate. "I couldn't eat another bite."

Andy grabbed her plate and pushed his empty one aside. "Well, I sure can." He took a fork full of pancakes.

"See ya." Mia stood up.

Andy held up his hand in a stop motion as he swallowed. "There is a little matter that I could use your help with."

"A little matter?"

"Okay, so it's not that little, but I need more privacy to explain." He picked up the plate containing Mia's uneaten food. "Let's go into Rick's office."

The owner was a friend of Andy's so no one stopped him from going past the "Employees Only" door. Following Andy into the owner's office, Mia hoped the job wasn't as big or complicated as the most recent one.

Andy flopped down into Rick's chair, set the plate on the desk, and proceeded to take a few more bites.

Mia closed the door behind her and took a seat on the other side of the desk.

"Sis, I'm in a bit of trouble. I know I promised the last job would be it, but things got somewhat out of hand."

"Somewhat?" Mia's blue eyes weren't smiling.

"Well." Andy scratched his head. "Well...the

diamonds…were short."

"Short? Did the guy who hired you misjudge the quantity?"

"Well." Andy's eyes avoided Mia's. "He knew how many there should have been. A few never made it to him."

Mia squinted. "A few? What did you do with them, Andy?"

"Wanted to pay off the mortgage on my shop. Thought I could make a few extra bucks on the side and he'd never know."

"What mortgage on your shop? You paid cash for it!"

"Thought I was on a lucky streak."

"Gambling? Andy, you swore that was behind you when I gave you the rest of the money to buy the shop."

"The missing diamonds need to be replaced, or I'm toast."

"Andy, we were paid well for that heist. My share of the money is tucked away. Can we pay for the missing diamonds?"

"Five mil?"

"Five million? Exactly how many diamonds didn't you deliver?"

"It wasn't that many. He's bumping up the replacement price to teach me a lesson."

"If only we knew where Dad put his stash. He never gave you a clue?"

"Nope. Never got him to even hint where he'd hidden his fortune. If he'd introduced me to some of his buyers, then we could get paid for the product instead of the job. More bucks that way. This problem wouldn't exist."

"Maybe we could steal back the diamonds you lost gambling. Who has those?"

"The last dude Dad hooked me up with. He wants me to snatch more."

"Let me see if I've got this right. You want us to steal diamonds for the same person that won the prior diamonds in a gambling game? That smells like a set up to me."

"I knew up front the dude wanted diamonds. He even examined them before we played."

"It still smells like a set up to me. He probably figured out where you got the diamonds before you were dealt the first hand. He sounds like a real con man. Not that the other guys we've worked for aren't, but they solicit you before the job. They don't pretend to come to your aid. Any of your other contacts need a job pulled?"

"I'm kind of in a time crunch."

"How much time have you got?"

"A week."

Mia exhaled. "Not enough time to plan let alone execute a delicate operation."

"J.D., the guy we did the job for, has already sold the uncut stones—the whole heist. The buyer is coming in town to pick them up on Wednesday, a week from tomorrow. J.D. wanted the cash or the replacements by Sunday, but I talked him into giving me a couple more days."

"He was cool with that?"

"Not happy, but dead men can't repay, and he'd rather have the five mil than my hide."

Mia stared at Andy. *If he's not too worried, he must know J.D. well. But five million can end a friendship.* She'd never met any of the men who hired Andy. All she knew about them was they were well connected and wore Armani suits. "Have we done other jobs for J.D.?"

"Yep. Quite a few. Guess that's why he's giving me a partial pass. He suggested the target. Dad never wanted you to know his contacts, so I'm not going to say anything more. It's for your protection."

Their father's buddies all knew Andy was his kid and believed he had hired a woman to help with some of his heists, but none of them suspected the woman was Leo Carlyle's daughter. Mia's father had given her a new identity. Since her mother loved the name Mia, he didn't change that, but her last name was changed. Mia Sloan's forged birth certificate showed she was born four months earlier than Mia Carlyle and in Los Angeles instead of New York.

Mia glanced at her watch. "I need to go. I'll only work half a day."

"Meet me at our usual place at one." A big smile came over Andy's face. "By the way, the new boss is going to pay my assistant a hundred grand. I'll scope out the target."

Returning a half smile, Mia rose and headed out the door. As she climbed into a cab, she didn't feel the sense of excitement. The thrill of pulling jobs had left after losing her father. She'd once believed the Carlyles were invincible and couldn't get caught. Every move was carefully laid out with all contingencies taken into consideration, except the last job with him. That was the first and only time gunshots had ever been fired during one of their heists. To this day, Mia still didn't know what had gone wrong. The cops showed up at her father's house two days after that job, the same day he intended to turn the merchandise over to the buyer.

At 9:35, Mia stepped out of the elevator on the twelfth floor, occupied by the advertising agency she worked for, Feinstein & Dawson. She walked toward her office and saw her boss, Blaine Feinstein, standing near her door.

"I was starting to think you weren't going to make it in today." The white-haired man in his early sixties waited for her reply.

"My aunt is sick again. I stopped by to see how she was doing. I'd like to take her to the doctor this afternoon. Will it be a problem if I leave early?"

"You can leave as soon as we get through with this morning's client pitch." He eyed her up and down. "You look great as always."

Mia was used to Feinstein checking her out whenever an important client or potential client was expected at the agency. She was never offended by it because he always treated her kindly. Since he and his wife were childless, they viewed the staff as their family. "Thank you. Do you want me to do anything for the presentation?"

"Just clinch the deal! The potential client specifically requested that you lead the agency team that would handle his account. If Lewis stumbles, help him out."

"Certainly."

Feinstein's nephew, Lewis, frequently got tongue-tied in the middle of a client presentation. Since Feinstein always gave his nephew that task, Mia figured Lewis was being groomed to take over someday.

When the time came to set up the presentation, Mia strolled into the conference room with Lewis.

She was surprised to see the potential client, a fifty-something man with heavy, black brows, had arrived early and was chatting and laughing with her boss about something.

Feinstein nodded to her. "Hank, let me introduce you to Mia…"

"That won't be necessary, Blaine." The man rubbed his prominent chin. "I remember Mia from the party at your house last month."

Feinstein often invited potential clients to his parties. This man owned Mercedes and BMW dealerships all over the state. *Winning his account could be worth millions of dollars to the agency.* She stretched out her hand. "Mr. Gunther, how are you?"

He shook her hand. "Mia, please call me Hank."

"Certainly, Hank."

A man and woman, each expensively clothed, came into the room and stood beside Hank. "These are my key managers." Hank introduced them to Blaine, Mia, and Lewis.

After the PowerPoint presentation appeared on the screen, Mia worked the computer while Lewis spoke. Occasionally, she glanced at Gunther to see his reaction to their pitch. His eyes were always focused on her. She knew men found her attractive, but she had never before been in the conference room where a potential client couldn't keep his eyes off her. They always at least appeared to be listening to the presenter. Then she recalled hearing that Gunther's wife died in a car crash a few years earlier. At the party, rumors flew that he was on the hunt for wife number two. *That is a role I have no interest in filling.*

Mia heard Lewis stuttering and snapped out of her contemplations. She stood. "Thanks, Lewis. This is my slide."

"Sorry, Mia. I got carried away." He always used the same line.

"No problem." Mia picked up where Lewis had left off. This time Gunther listened to every word she said, but she sensed the man had the same ulterior motive as most men on the prowl. She vowed that he'd never get what he wanted from her.

Chapter 2

Surrounded by thick foliage of bushes and trees, Andy sat at their usual bench, thumbing through a magazine.

"Sorry, I wasn't able to get here earlier." Mia, breathless and flushed, took a seat next to her brother. "The meeting lasted much longer than I expected. Have you been here long?"

"Almost an hour, but I knew you'd show."

"Okay. I'm assuming you've scoped out the place."

"Yep. Did that last night. Even made a quick visit."

"You broke in?"

"Like I said, there's a time crunch. From the way the new dude talked about the safe and layout, thought I could go solo on this. But the safe didn't have any uncut stones in it. Plenty of cash, trays of jewelry, and cut diamonds."

"Did you take anything?"

"Nope. Didn't want anyone to know I had paid a

visit. Security wasn't that tight. It sure would be moved up a notch or two if anything had gone missing."

"Could the place have two safes?"

"Not that I could find. You'll have to do it."

"You're an expert in locating safes. How do you expect me to do it?"

"Probably what we're looking for is in his house."

"Any possibility the guy doesn't *have* any uncut diamonds? That he's sold them to someone else?"

"Not a chance. He's the final purchaser. He has the equipment and personally cuts them."

"A jeweler?"

"Yep. Oliver LeMonte."

Mia thought for a moment. "He owns jewelry stores at high end spots in the U.S., France, and the U.K. Maybe he's sent the diamonds to another location."

"Nope. He's in New York, and that's where the new dude says the diamonds are. He fronted me twenty grand to take care of expenses. He wouldn't do that if he had any doubt."

"If the plan is for me to get cozy with LeMonte, there isn't enough time. Usually, one of us stakes out the mark for at least a couple of weeks to observe his routine before I *accidentally* bump into him. Here I thought I'd be drawing the attention of a security guard, disabling security systems, keeping a look out, something like that…not enticing the mark."

"Sis, he lives in a walled-off estate. LeMonte has one or two security guards at his place most of the time. The heist is going to have to be a quick in-and-out. No time to go searching for the safe."

"Andy, I don't know who this new boss is, but he

shouldn't have led you to one of LeMonte's stores to steal the diamonds when the mark's house is set up like a fortress. Since you broke into the store without having to study all the bells and whistles of the security system, unless LeMonte isn't all that clever, he wouldn't leave a stash of uncut diamonds there."

"The store safe is a huge Underwood and tough to crack. No amateur could've handled it or hauled it away."

"But cracking safes is your specialty."

"Diamond cutting equipment is in the basement of his store. That's probably why the dude figured the stones would be there. Eventually, they'll show up there."

Mia smiled at Andy. "Given your time constraints, you want me to ask him when they'll show up there? That might be easier than asking him where the safe is in his house."

"Wow. Could you do that, Sis?"

"Seriously, Andy, I don't even know if I could finagle a way to get him to invite me to his home that quickly. That isn't how I operate."

Andy rubbed Mia's arm. "You're smooth and cool. Set it up so the mark believes he had to work hard to get you to go home with him."

"Any possibility you could get J.D. to give you another week?"

Andy pressed his lips together and shook his head. "Nope. I was pushing it to get a few more days."

"Do you really think he'd whack you if you didn't come through?"

"Yes. Even if he likes our work, not collecting his due would be viewed as a sign of weakness."

"But he'd get zero then."

"It wouldn't be the first time he left money on the table."

"Okay. Tell me about Oliver LeMonte."

Andy pulled out his cell and tapped on it several times. Holding it up, he said, "That's him. I snapped it today."

Mia took his phone and studied the picture. A handsome man in his mid thirties with dark hair and deep brown eyes, LeMonte had a nice, pleasant expression on his face.

"He's a little over six feet tall and has an athletic build. When I stopped near the gate of his estate this morning before breakfast, he jogged right by me. Could be his daily exercise routine."

"Married?"

"Divorce was finalized a couple of months ago. From what I understand, the ex-wife took him to the cleaners."

"Does he work in the store, or is he a behind-the-scenes sort of owner?"

"Don't have a clue. Thought about going there to find out, but I'd have to wear a suit to pretend I could afford that type of jewelry. Guys in oil-stained jeans, t-shirts, and tattoos don't fit the mold." His raised an eyebrow. "You, however, look like a gal that shops in high-end places."

"Think he'll give me a free sample?"

"If you play your cards right, you might get something worth keeping."

"I have to attend a fundraiser Friday night."

"Can you get out of it?"

"No. Feinstein is on the Southeast Hospital board. He reserved three tables at the event, and I promised him I'd attend. I'll leave right after dinner."

Andy sighed in resignation. "This job is going to require burner phones. I'll get 'em. Stop by LeMonte's store this afternoon and see if you can catch his eye."

"Okay. Meet me at Sammy's around seven, and I'll let you know how it went."

Sammy's wasn't a high class bar, but they often frequented it to discuss business. Their dad had drummed into them that they should never go to each other's places. He didn't want any possibility they could be linked. Even though he was gone, they still followed his advice. So they met at private spots in public places and never went or left together. The only times they moved around together were when they were doing a job, and that always occurred under the cover of darkness.

Mia gazed at LeMonte's Fine Jewelry as the cab crawled along in slow traffic. Its elegant granite and glass façade attracted her eye. She hated the thought of having to quickly stir up a relationship with a complete stranger, but she loved her brother and knew he'd never hesitate to help her out if she found herself in a jam. Andy dealt with hard-core criminals, where Mia had always been in the background. Andy had promised there wouldn't be any more night jobs after he got his shop, but Mia knew from the onset he couldn't keep that promise. Andy had vices. Gambling was on top of the list. But she loved him.

Mia paid the cabbie and headed into LeMonte's. She liked to shop on Fifth Avenue with her ill-gotten earnings, a luxury that would end when she had to rely only on her salary. She was willing to give that up in order to avoid being caught, going to prison, and possibly ending up like her father.

Stepping through LeMonte's doorway, Mia saw the man in the picture behind the counter, helping a customer select a ring. She smiled to herself, knowing a minor hurdle had been resolved. LeMonte was accessible to customers, not a behind-the-scenes owner as she'd feared. Gazing through the glass cases, Mia was entranced by the exquisite jewelry.

A well-dressed, middle-aged woman, wearing an unusual sapphire brooch, approached Mia. "May I help you?"

"What a lovely pin." Mia gestured toward it.

"Thank you. Our sapphire jewelry is in the case at the other end of the counter. Would you like to see some of the pieces?"

Noticing that area was close to the place where LeMonte was assisting an elderly man, Mia nodded and followed the saleswoman.

"You've made an excellent choice, Mr. Fillmore." LeMonte wrote on a notepad. "Your wife's birthday is Thursday. We'll have it sized to fit her delicate hand. Would you like to pick it up, or should we deliver it to your office?"

"I'll have my assistant pick it up."

Watching the two men shake hands, and then seeing Fillmore leave, Mia contemplated how she could get LeMonte to wait on her instead of the saleswoman.

A banging and pounding came through a door behind the counter.

LeMonte glanced at Mia and a faint smile crossed his lips.

An odd tingling sensation spread through her body. *Have I met him before?*

He turned to the saleswoman and tilted his head

toward the noise. "Marilyn, can you check on their progress? I'll take care of this customer."

"Certainly." The woman opened the door behind her and left the room.

"Sorry about the commotion, Miss Sloan."

Mia was taken aback. "How do you know my name?"

"I saw you at a party last spring hosted by Feinstein & Dawson."

Mia prided herself on never forgetting the names of those who were invited to company parties, but she couldn't recall ever seeing the name LeMonte on any guest list. "Did you enjoy the party?"

"Yes. You don't remember me, do you?"

"I'm sorry, Mr. LeMonte." Mia noticed his eyes slightly narrowing and wondered if he expected her to call him by his first name, but she couldn't recall ever talking to the man, so she returned his formality. "There were a lot of people at the party, and obviously my memory is not as good as yours."

He smiled. "That's understandable. We never spoke. I was there for less than an hour, and LeMonte's Fine Jewelry is not currently one of your clients."

"Currently? Does that mean you are considering becoming one?"

"Yes. Feinstein has been courting me for almost six months. We're not pleased with our advertising agency."

"Feinstein & Dawson has an excellent reputation for creative concepts. Perhaps we can give you a tour of our offices and a presentation." Mia almost lost track of the purpose for her visit. *I'm not here as a Feinstein employee. I'm here to help my brother.* "But I am curious. Since we never spoke at the party, how do you know my name?"

"I asked Lewis Feinstein. He's a longtime customer of ours."

Mia knew Lewis had good taste. He always wore perfectly tailored Armani suits. Despite becoming tongue-tied in meetings, he dressed immaculately.

A crashing sound emanated from the other side of the wall behind him.

"Please excuse me for a moment." His eyes moved to a salesman who was putting a tray full of rings back into a counter. "Ralph, please take care of Miss Sloan until I return."

LeMonte went through the door behind the counter, and Ralph stepped to the other side of the counter in front of Mia.

Mia had him show her some of the sapphire rings while her eyes kept glancing at the door, waiting for LeMonte to return. She was busy admiring the tenth ring she had placed on her finger, a square-shaped sapphire surrounded by diamonds, when LeMonte finally stepped out of the back room.

"Thank you, Ralph." LeMonte moved to the counter.

Ralph left to help another customer.

"That took a little longer than I anticipated." His eyes dropped to her finger. "That ring doesn't do your hand justice, Miss Sloan. Let me show you something else." He lifted a ring, which had an oval sapphire and diamonds twice the size of the ring on her finger, out of the glass case.

Still hearing noise coming from behind the door, Mia asked, "Are you having some remodeling done in your office?"

"No." LeMonte gently removed the ring from her finger.

She had never experienced a jeweler who did that before.

"We had a break-in last night, and we're having some additional security equipment installed."

Could Andy have slipped up and left traces behind? "Did the burglar get away with a lot of jewels?"

"Yes, along with a significant amount of cash. It's been a real eye-opener that our old security system was not up to par with our needs. Now the authorities will be alerted if any unauthorized person enters the office, whether it's during store hours or after closing."

"Oh, how terrible to suffer such a theft." *Andy lied to me.* He claimed he hadn't taken anything. If the uncut diamonds end up back at the store, it's going to be appreciably harder to swipe them. Stealing them within a week was already going to be a difficult task, and now Mia wondered if the task had become impossible. In the past, she and Andy had always studied the type of security system in place and determined how to override it. *Maybe we'd be better off trying to find another source of uncut diamonds or stealing five million dollars.*

Mia decided she'd have to talk to Andy about that. Even though she was still furious with him, she didn't want any harm to come to her brother.

LeMonte slipped the other ring on her finger. "Perfect fit. You were meant to have this ring, Miss Sloan."

She gazed at the beautiful stones and had to admit it looked awesome on her finger, but buying a ring when she needed five million dollars was out of the question. "It certainly is lovely, but I'm afraid it's more than I can afford." Mia began to take it off.

LeMonte laid his hand on top of hers. "Wear it for a few days, and if you still like it, I'm sure we can arrange a payment scenario for you."

"Mr. LeMonte, that's very generous of you, but I couldn't possibly accept that offer."

Keeping his hand on hers so she couldn't remove the ring, he said, "Miss Sloan, I insist. And if the ring ends up missing or stolen, we have insurance to take care of those contingencies."

Was he inferring I should just keep it? Mia had never had such a spectacular piece of jewelry, and she wasn't about to disappoint LeMonte. She'd need him unless Andy could find another solution for the problem. "Thank you, Mr. LeMonte. I'll treasure it for a few days."

"My pleasure, Miss Sloan." He rubbed her hand before releasing it. "Would you care to have dinner with me tomorrow evening?"

He's fast. He's handsome. But maybe, since his divorce, he doesn't have much of a social life. It normally takes me longer for a mark to ask me out. LeMonte is making it too easy for me. "That will give me a wonderful opportunity to show off this ring."

"Eight o'clock?"

She nodded.

More loud bangs came from behind the door.

LeMonte glanced over his shoulder. "See you then. I need to check on their progress."

Chapter 3

Shortly before seven, Mia arrived at Sammy's and glanced around but couldn't see Andy anywhere. Their favorite booth, farthest away from the entrance and with utmost privacy, was free. She sat down and ordered a glass of wine.

When Andy walked in, Mia was working on her second glass. He slipped into the booth. "Sorry I'm late. Had a little trouble at the shop."

"What kind of trouble?"

He waved his hand. "Nothing to do with that." Andy slid a phone across the table. "My number's in it, and yours is in mine."

Mia dropped the burner phone in her purse. "So what was the problem at the shop?"

"Seems a new employee lied on his application. Claimed to be an experienced mechanic. Turned out the guy only knew how to change tires but attempted to change fan belts. Big mistake. Customer needed his wheels, so I took over. I canned him, so now I'm down a mechanic." Andy signaled to the barmaid.

"Sam Adams."

After Andy took his first swig, Mia said, "Well, your ex-employee isn't the only liar working at your shop."

A puzzled look flashed on Andy's face. "Another employee? How do you know that?"

"I don't know your employees, but I do know their boss, the guy who lied to me earlier today."

"What are you talking about?"

Mia leaned closer to her brother and softly said, "You told me that you didn't take anything from the safe, but you did. LeMonte is having a new security system installed because last night someone broke into their safe, stealing cash and jewelry."

Andy shook his head. "Honest, Sis, I didn't take anything. The diamonds weren't in there. I locked up the safe and searched for another one. I thought the diamonds would end up there soon—to be cut. Easier to swipe them from the store than his fortress."

"Now the store is probably rigged to the hilt, just like LeMonte's house. No unauthorized person can enter the office."

"All codes can be overridden."

"With time." Mia fumed. She tilted her head and her face scrunched up in uncertainty. "Wait a minute. You're telling me that you didn't take anything?"

"Sis, I swear. Nothing. Nada."

"You broke in last night. And you took nothing? Then what happened to LeMonte's cash and jewels?"

Andy grimaced. "Jesus! Someone else is after the loot. I was careful but didn't have a lookout. I broke one of Dad's rules. I didn't cover my ass because I didn't want to get you involved. Our boss on this job made it sound simple."

"Maybe the thief isn't after the same stuff we're after."

Andy frowned. "Whoever broke in had to be a pro. Doubt if there was more than ten grand in cash, and LeMonte's jewelry is unique, easy to identify…difficult to fence."

"If that thief was a pro after the diamonds, then why was anything taken? That person is going to be faced with the same problem we're faced with now."

"I don't have an answer. Unless he figured there was no way to break into the fortress and taking some loot was better than nothing. Was everything in the safe taken?"

"Not according to LaMonte." Mia leaned forward. "Do you think your new boss hired someone else to snatch the diamonds, in case we couldn't get the job done?"

"Not likely. The dude fronted me twenty grand for expenses."

"Great. Now we need to worry about getting to the prize before our unknown competition."

"Back to the basics. How did it go with LeMonte?"

Mia held up her hand to show off the ring. "He gave me this to wear for a few days."

Andy took her hand and stared at the ring. "Just like that? I knew you were good, but Sis, you've raised the bar. No other gal could get a guy to give her a ring like that after only one meeting." He raised an eyebrow. "How much time did you spend with him?"

"Come on, Andy. No private time. I just talked to him in the store, but he recognized me from one of Feinstein's parties."

"So the poor guy's been pining for you ever since?"

"We have a date tomorrow night."

"Wow. Here I was worried you might not be able to move that relationship along quickly." Andy grinned. "Sorry, Sis. I underestimated your ability. Can you get him to invite you to his house tomorrow?"

"We'll just have to see how it goes. I do have to play a little hard-to-get."

"Not for long." Andy looked at his watch. "I need to get back to the shop to figure out what else the bozo screwed up. Only a few companies supply and install the type of security equipment LeMonte most likely had installed. I intend to pay them a visit tomorrow. My shop could use a sophisticated security system."

"Right. Wouldn't want anyone to steal a can of oil or a bolt."

"Come on, Sis. If someone broke in, they'd at least take a wrench or a screwdriver."

Mia twisted strands of brown hair around her finger, a nervous habit that helped her keep a poker face. "So you'll be guarding the place tonight, watching out for burglars, until you get that sophisticated security system installed?"

"That's the way it's got to be." Andy stood. "Call me after your date."

"Will do."

Mia waited another fifteen minutes before leaving. Walking to her car, she had an eerie feeling. *Is someone watching me?* She saw no one but heard footsteps. Mia slipped her hand inside her purse, pulled out her Beretta Pico .380, and released the safety. With her other hand, she retrieved her car keys and pushed the button to unlock the doors. She quickly slid inside, laid her pistol on the passenger seat, turned on the ignition, and heard the locks snap in place. In the side mirror, she spotted a figure, wearing a hoodie, ducking between cars.

Pulling out, she noticed the headlights of another vehicle in her rear view mirror. Assuming the driver was the hoodie-clad figure, Mia made a series of turns on red lights, constantly checking her mirror for the tail. She noticed a black BMW, but each time she thought she could catch the plate number, it slowed down. There were lots of black BMWs in the city, so she couldn't be sure it was always the same one. She drove into her apartment building's garage. The gate closed behind her, but she spotted one black BMW pulling over to the curb across from her building.

As soon as she reached the lobby and saw the concierge, Mia sighed with relief, got her mail, and took the secure elevator to her floor.

Once inside her place, she bolted the door. Her personal cell ringtone sounded. Glancing at the screen, she saw "unidentified caller." Mia didn't answer. If it was important, the caller would leave a message.

After getting a bottle of water, Mia looked through the mail and then saw a voice mail message on her phone from "unidentified caller." She tapped on it.

An unfamiliar male voice said, "Mia, Mia, Mia. Why you?"

What's that supposed to mean?

While mulling that over, Mia took a shower and got ready for bed. As she started to fall asleep, her cell rang. The screen showed "unidentified caller" again.

She adjusted her pillow and turned away. No message beep sounded.

* * *

It was almost lunchtime the next day when Lewis strolled into Mia's office. "I noticed your ring in the break room. Did you buy it at LeMonte's, or is it from a new admirer?"

Lewis frequently asked her out and pried into her social life. She figured he was probably curious if she was still available.

"No new admirers. You know I want to focus on my career, and I have to look after my aunt. The ring is from LeMonte's, but I haven't decided if I can afford it yet."

Lewis narrowed his eyes. "LeMonte let you walk out of the store without paying for it?"

"Yes, on loan to decide. I'll return it in a few days if I don't buy it."

"Can I take a closer look?"

"Sure." Mia removed the ring and handed it to him.

He held it five or six inches from his eyes. "These are very fine stones. Not that LeMonte would ever sell a low-grade gem, but there are degrees of quality. This is top-notch."

"How do you know that?"

"I trained to be a jeweler in Belgium for two years. Everything changed when my dad had his accident. I returned to the states and came to work here."

Mia knew Lewis's father had fallen into a drained swimming pool and sustained a serious head injury that left him partially paralyzed and unable to speak.

Before that, his father had been an executive at the agency. Now, Mia saw Lewis in a more sympathetic light. He'd given up his dream. No wonder he struggled giving presentations. They had something in common—she'd never wanted a life of crime, but now she'd have a hard time walking away from it. "Maybe you could still be a jeweler."

"That ship has sailed. My future is with Feinstein & Dawson." He smiled. "You certainly know how to make us look good to clients."

Mia blushed slightly before returning his smile. "Thanks."

He held up the ring. "I have an account with LeMonte's. I could probably finagle you a good discount."

"Well, I'm leaning toward returning it."

Lewis handed back the ring. "Let me know if you change your mind. Oh, I almost forgot what I came in here for in the first place. Hank Gunther liked the presentation. He wants to see it again but this time geared toward BMWs instead of the Mercedes line. I have some staff members working on that. They'll have it ready to go this afternoon so we can watch it with the boss in the conference room for any final tweaks."

"What time?"

"Three."

After Lewis left, Mia replayed in her mind the prior day's presentation. She didn't think Gunther had even paid attention to it, except her part, and wondered if he was coming in for another reason—to see her.

The beginning part of the afternoon seemed to drag as the image of LeMonte kept flashing into Mia's head. She couldn't deny her attraction to the man, but going out with him was strictly to obtain information. She had never fallen for a mark before, and she wasn't about ready to let LeMonte get under her skin. If that should happen, she feared she might hesitate stealing from him. Her goal was to help Andy, not succumb to her own desires. *Maybe still seeing LeMonte after Andy's problem has been resolved might not be a bad idea.*

At 3:05 p.m., Mia sat in the conference room next to Feinstein, and Lewis clicked on the PowerPoint presentation.

When the image of a black BMW appeared on the screen, Mia's gut clenched. *Could the driver of the BMW that I thought followed me last night be the unidentified caller? And was it someone who saw me with Andy in the bar?*

"What do you think, Mia?" Feinstein's question snapped her out of her contemplations.

"It looks good," she said, though she hadn't been paying attention.

Feinstein agreed. "Then we're all set for tomorrow's ten o'clock with Mr. Gunther."

Mia returned to her office and saw a note on her desk. It read, "Your mechanic called. The part he ordered for your car came in."

She guessed "the mechanic" was her brother, and he wanted to talk to her. She pulled the burner phone out of her purse to check for a message for him. No calls. No messages. Andy had sometimes called her at work on her direct line but never on a company phone answered by another employee. Thinking maybe he had lost his burner phone and hadn't memorized her burner number, Mia stuck that phone in her pocket and took the elevator down to the main lobby. Standing in the corner, a distance from anyone who might overhear, she called her brother.

"What's up?" he answered.

"That's just what I was going to ask you. Why did you call me at work?"

"Huh? I didn't call you."

"Andy, someone called and left a message claiming to be my mechanic."

"It wasn't me. Someone is snooping around. I'll see what I can find out. You still on for your date?"

"Yes."

"What time?"

"Eight."

"If I learn anything, I'll call you before I go. But Sis, make sure this LeMonte fella walks you into your building. Don't be alone anywhere. Something is going on, and I don't like it."

"Something is definitely going on," Mia said and then briefed Andy on the strange phone calls, the guy in the hoodie in Sammy's parking lot, and the BMW she thought had followed her home.

"Not good. I'm seeing one of Dad's buddies tomorrow. Maybe he can help sort this out or point me in the right direction."

"Be careful, Andy."

"Yeah, my ass is already on the line. Not a good time to make new enemies." Andy disconnected.

Back at her desk, Mia worried what Andy might do. Like her father, Andy had a ruthless side. Anyone who ever crossed their father, Leo, was never given a second chance, and Andy followed that creed. She guessed he had spent a large part of his day trying to hunt down his rival. And she knew exactly how Andy would handle someone muscling in on his gig.

Chapter 4

Nervously applying makeup for her date, Mia wished Andy would call with an update. Having to constantly monitor her surroundings for unsavory characters could interfere with her enticement of LeMonte, which needed total focus.

A few minutes past eight, the concierge called her apartment and told her that a Mr. LeMonte had arrived.

"Thank you. I'll be right down." Mia had never spent time with a mark on her turf, and she didn't intend to make an exception for LeMonte.

When she stepped out of the elevator, LeMonte walked toward her, his eyes revealing appreciation for what he saw. "Good evening, Miss Sloan."

"Mr. LeMonte, please call me Mia."

"I will, if you'll call me Oliver."

"Certainly, Oliver." Mia felt flushed but projected a cool demeanor.

He led her to a silver Alfa Romeo parked by the curb and opened the passenger door.

Mia's nostrils were permeated by the distinctive new-car smell as she slid into the seat. She glanced at its sleek interior while LeMonte looped around the vehicle's hood, opened his door, and sat behind the wheel.

He edged into the traffic. "Do you still like the ring?"

"Yes, very much." Mia checked the side mirror for a tail. "But I've come to a final conclusion that it is more than I can afford."

"How do you know? You never asked the price."

"I can tell just from looking at it. No need to ask the price." She bit the inside of her lip. "But I intend to keep it for a few more days as per your offer."

"Good. Maybe I can change your mind."

Mia loved the ring, but buying an expensive piece of jewelry would eat into her reserves. Dropping a large wad of cash could easily also draw unwanted attention. She changed the subject. "Are the police making any progress in locating the burglar who broke into your store?"

"No. The fingerprints they lifted off of the safe belonged to either Vince or me. Vince is my cousin and a silent partner in the business."

Mia kept watching for a tail as she and LeMonte talked about his store while they drove. When they pulled onto the expressway, she became concerned. "Oliver, where are you taking me? I thought we were going to a restaurant."

"I just got back from Paris, and I see too many people who want to dominate my time in a restaurant. I have a professional chef on staff. He's preparing Beef Wellington for us. And don't worry, you'll be safe at my home."

It solved her problem of having to watch out for a too interested stranger lurking around her, and besides spending time with a highly attractive man, she could scope out the place for a safe.

LeMonte turned into a driveway and a wrought-iron gate opened. He drove through the archway. The large private courtyard with a circular drive led to a two-story stone house.

Mia gasped. "This is so well hidden....I can't believe it's in the city."

"The outer walls conceal it as just another old building. It was built in the early 19th century by a speculator who went bust. My great-grandfather picked it up for the mortgage. But now it has the most up-to-date fixtures and security that money can buy."

Mia noticed an armed guard standing near the corner of the house and a dark green Mercedes and a black BMW parked near a four-car garage. She gestured toward the vehicles. "Will there be other guests?"

"No."

As Mia walked across the threshold, she heard a faint beep, glanced up, and caught a glimpse of a security camera partially concealed in the entry hall's hanging light fixture. She already assumed all of the entrances and windows were hooked up to a security system and wondered if guards constantly monitored the cameras or if everything was recorded to be viewed only when a disturbance occurred in the house.

An ornate stairwell dominated the entry hall beyond grand archways, opening into a living room on one side and a dining room on the other. Mia was surprised to see the table hadn't been set.

LeMonte led her into the living room. "Would you care for a glass of wine before dinner?"

"Yes, Merlot, if you have it."

He smiled. "Exactly what I guessed."

Mia wondered if he already knew her preference.

LeMonte motioned Mia to take a seat in front of the fireplace. Even though it wasn't a cold evening, a small fire burned in it. He poured two glasses of wine and handed her one.

"Thank you." Mia took a sip. "This Merlot is exquisite." She scanned the room with original artwork and the latest Italian furniture. "You have a lovely home, Oliver."

"It's been passed down for three generations and belongs to the entire family, not just me. I stay here when I'm in New York, but often another family member shows up. Fortunately, no one else is in town. Otherwise, we wouldn't be dining here."

"Do you come from a large family?" The research she had done on Oliver LeMonte didn't indicate he had any siblings. If she were to lure him away the night Andy would break in, she had to warn her brother that in addition to worrying about the guards, family members might also be a concern.

"No. Most have passed. I have three cousins, an aunt, and uncle."

"You're an only child?"

"I did have…" LeMonte abruptly stopped and a sad expression flashed on his face. Then he picked up the bottle of wine and filled their glasses.

His reaction had piqued her curiosity. *Did he have a sibling who died?*

"How about you, Mia? Do you come from a large

family?"

She shook her head. "No. I'm an only child. My parents died when I was young, and my aunt raised me." Mia had told the false story for so long, it had become an automatic response. "My aunt is still alive but not in good health."

"Oh, I'm sorry to hear that." LeMonte glanced at his watch and then stood. "We're having dinner on the balcony."

Mia took his cue and rose to her feet.

As he led her down the hallway, he pointed out his ancestors in the portraits hanging on the wall.

Half-listening, Mia looked for security equipment. She noticed two surveillance cameras in the crown molding and was impressed by how well they were hidden.

LeMonte guided her through a room that had a huge television screen that covered half of one wall. Comfortable-looking couches and chairs were situated in front of it. He took her out a balcony door to a round table, elegantly set for two.

Mia sat down, glancing over the railing at the fountain in the center of an immaculately manicured lawn surrounded by flowers and bushes. "Oh, it's lovely out here."

"Before my grandmother made this her permanent residence, the yard only consisted of grass and a few trees. She had it all changed. It's stayed that way ever since."

"She created a lovely spot. It's perfect."

A door at the other end of the balcony opened. A middle-aged man wearing a white apron carried a tray with covered plates and placed one in front of each of them, along with a basket filled with rolls. Then he filled their wine goblets and removed the lids covering the food, saying "*Bon appétit.*"

"Hope you like Caesar salad." LeMonte put a napkin on his lap.

"I do."

They spoke very little while eating their salads. Each time Mia glanced at LeMonte, she sensed from the way his eyes were fixed on her face that he was studying her. Whenever he met her eyes, a faint smile crossed his lips, and then he directed his gaze into the yard while he ate another bite.

The minute they finished their salads, a gray-haired maid came out and cleared away their plates.

Mia spotted two clearly visible surveillance cameras were attached to the house above the corners of the balcony. Since the plates had been so promptly removed, she suspected they were being watched.

The middle-aged man returned with the main course.

Mia smiled at the chef. "The Beef Wellington looks delicious."

While they ate, LeMonte asked, "How long have you worked for Feinstein & Dawson?"

"Going on six years," Mia said, between bites.

"Where did you work before that?"

"Part-time for a small agency that only did billboards, and I took care of my aunt."

"How does she manage now?"

"A woman stays with her. I often drop by to make sure she's getting along okay, and she relies on me to take her to doctor appointments."

He finished off the wine in his glass. "Where does she live?"

Mia felt like he was interrogating her. Feinstein

had never asked that question. "In a small apartment on East 75th Street." She forced a smile. "Are you planning to visit her?"

"No. I was just wondering if she lived close to your place."

Moving the conversation away from her, Mia asked, "Where do you spend most of your time? In the States or in Europe?"

"In Paris, but after seeing you at Feinstein's party, I regretted having to immediately return to Paris."

"And why did you have to return?"

"A problem arose at the store there that needed my personal attention."

"Are any of your relatives planning to visit while you're here?"

"No one has mentioned it. The house has enough bedrooms to accommodate all of us plus some friends, so it wouldn't be a problem."

This additional uncertainty plagued Mia. Being aware of the potential number of people on the premises always had to be taken into consideration in the planning stages of any heist. *That was Dad's mistake. Maybe it would be easier to steal from the store than the house, but I can't ask Oliver when he's going to move uncut diamonds to the store safe.*

When they finished eating, LeMonte said, "I always enjoy showing off the house. Would you like a tour?"

"Yes. Very much." Mia thought LeMonte was doing a wonderful job in unknowingly helping her to locate the safe. Then she wondered if the whole tour was his way of getting women upstairs and into his bedroom. He had made it clear he was attracted to her, or maybe, he knew how to flawlessly deliver lines that rendered good results. Gazing at his handsome face, she couldn't imagine he needed to play games in order to get what he wanted. And his wealth would always attract women.

"Would you like to have dessert now or after the tour?"

"The meal was delicious. Please give my compliments to your chef. I couldn't eat another bite. I'm going to pass on dessert, but I would like to use your powder room."

"First door on the left in the hallway."

Mia walked through the room at the back of the house into the hallway. Instead of opening the first door on the left, she *accidentally* opened the one on the right. Seeing a stairwell leading to a basement with a light on at the bottom, she quickly closed the door and went into the bathroom across the hall. With surveillance cameras in the hallway, she knew her image had been captured and hoped it would be viewed as nothing more than her opening the wrong door.

When she returned to the table, LeMonte asked, "Will you join me for a glass of port after I've shown you the house?"

"I'd like that."

LeMonte escorted her back into the house. "This is the back parlor where people gather to watch television and chat."

As he spoke, Mia scanned the room for surveillance cameras. Two were concealed in the crown molding. LeMonte startled her by taking her hand.

He guided her past the door she had "accidentally" opened to the next closed door. LeMonte opened it and led her into a den. *A good place for a safe.* While he talked about the window coverings from Paris and the antique furnishings, Mia checked for security equipment. The room only had one surveillance camera. She ran her eyes around the doorframe, searching for a sign that indicated it had been wired for an alarm. Nothing stood out.

"You've already seen the front parlor." He directed her toward the dining room.

Walking into the room, she studied the archway and spotted small dots, not bigger than a tip of a pen, on the walls. The dots blended well with the textured wall. Mia had often seen laser security systems and knew the laser light beams would criss-cross the doorway when the alarm was activated. Based on the number of dots, the beams would only leave small open spaces between them. Unless the system was disabled, no one could enter the room without setting off the alarm. *Something important is in this room.* Her eyes drifted to a door on the adjacent wall.

"The butler's pantry and kitchen are through there," LeMonte said, and Mia figured he had noticed her staring at the door. "I don't include that in the tour."

"Could I peek in?"

He nodded toward it. "Be my guest."

As Mia opened the door, she checked out the door frame. It had small dots embedded in the wood frame in front of the door. She quickly glanced into the butler's pantry. The door between it and the kitchen stood wide open, and she saw the back of the maid near the sink. Closing the door, she said, "Big kitchen. It's set up to handle a crowd."

"It takes care of our needs."

She identified two additional concealed surveillance cameras in the dining room. From where they were positioned, it appeared one camera pointed toward the archway and the other toward the wall containing the door to the butler's pantry. Mia wandered around the room, stopping and admiring each painting, as she tried to determine which one hid the safe.

LeMonte walked by her side, naming each artist and explaining how each painting had been acquired. Some had been purchased at auctions and a few had been commissioned.

When Mia reached the fourth painting which was against the same wall as the pantry door, she noticed the picture frame was thicker and slightly wider than the other frames. Given the size of the paintings in the room, a picture frame would have to be hinged in order to obtain easy access to a safe behind it. The room had no windows. A fireplace with a mirror above it occupied the center of the wall opposite that painting.

Leading Mia up an ornate stairwell to the second floor, LeMonte discussed the hand-carved posts. Upstairs, he took her to the far end of the hallway and began to show her each bedroom. All the bedrooms had en suite bathrooms. The furnishings ranged from heavy, rustic pine to antiques to ultra-modern. "Each member of the family personally selected the furnishings for their rooms, so all the styles are different. The three bedrooms with traditional furnishings are for guests."

The last room they entered was LeMonte's. It had the latest European modern furnishings.

"What do you think?" LeMonte asked as Mia

looked around.

"Surprised that you selected modern furniture. I had anticipated that you'd go the traditional route."

He took off his blazer, dropped it in a chair and stepped closer to her. "Mia, there is a lot you don't know about me, and there's a lot I don't know about you."

As his brown eyes meet hers, an unexpected desire surged through her body.

A sensuous smile crossed his lips, and he enveloped her in his arms and kissed her. "I've wanted to do that since the first time I saw you." He held her closer and kissed her again.

Feeling his muscular chest through his shirt, she kissed him back and wrapped her arms around his neck. As he deepened the kiss, a tingling sensation erupted down her spine.

He slowly began unzipping her dress.

Her breath came in wild gasps from anticipation. Then suddenly, unwelcome thoughts snapped into Mia's mind. *I can't let this happen. He's a mark. This is probably how he planned the evening to end. A one-night stand won't work. I have to play hard to get. Keeping a man lusting for me can be a valuable tool, a tool I might need to lure LeMonte away from his home or store.*

She forced herself to push him away. "Oliver, I don't jump into any man's bed without establishing a relationship first." She zipped up her dress. "I suspected you might have an alternative motive when you suggested that I keep the ring for a few days, but I had hoped I was wrong." Mia slipped off the ring and placed it on his bureau. "I don't want you to think that I owe you something."

LeMonte reached out for her. She backed away.

"Come on, Mia, that wasn't…"

She interrupted him. "Oliver, this might be your MO—loan a gorgeous ring or another piece of jewelry, have a romantic dinner on the balcony, give the woman a tour, and then end up in your bed. I'm afraid you've targeted the wrong woman for this evening's conquest."

"Mia, you've got me wrong. Yes, I wanted to make love to you, but this isn't some kind of game. I don't entertain a string of women, and I certainly don't loan out jewelry for that purpose. In fact, you are the only woman that I've *ever* allowed to walk out the door of any of my stores without paying for the piece of LeMonte jewelry she's wearing." He picked up the ring. "Please, take it back."

Mia shook her head. "Take me home."

He studied her face. "Can I sway you to still join me in a glass of port?"

"No. Maybe you'd rather I call a taxi."

"No. I'll take you home."

On the way out of the house, Mia retrieved her purse from the front parlor. Neither one of them spoke as LeMonte drove to her apartment building.

The minute he stopped in the only free space along the curb, almost a block from her building, Mia jumped out the passenger door and walked away at a brisk pace. She sensed LeMonte following her.

When she was only a few buildings away from hers, a man leapt out from between the parked cars and grabbed Mia's arm. Recalling Andy's warning not to be alone, Mia saw no weapon in the man's hand. She swung around, gripped his forearm, twisted it, leaned into him, and flipped him to the sidewalk. In the process, the thug wearing a ski mask released her arm. As her assailant staggered to stand and Mia swayed to regain her footing, LeMonte grabbed her attacker and punched him.

At lightning speed, the man squirmed out of LeMonte's grasp, charged down the sidewalk, and vanished among the people exiting a restaurant.

"Are you okay?" LeMonte reached for Mia.

Even though she felt a little shaken by the incident and would've liked the comfort his arms could've provided, she stepped beyond his reach. "Mr. LeMonte, thank you for coming to my rescue, but I am quite capable of taking care of myself."

"That I saw, and please call me Oliver."

Ignoring his request, Mia began walking toward her building.

He headed in the same direction, a few feet away from her. "I didn't realize unsavory characters roamed your neighborhood."

"Unsavory characters can be found anywhere in this town. Remember, your store on Fifth Avenue was recently robbed, and I doubt that was done by an upstanding member of society."

"Good point."

When the doorman opened the door for her, LeMonte asked, "Mia, will you consider going out with me again?"

Without turning around, she answered, "I'll have to think about that." Mia entered her building, and the doorman closed the door behind her.

Chapter 5

Mia tossed and turned all night after the attack. Before leaving for the office, her burner phone rang.

"Meet me at Sammy's when you get off work."

"Last night a guy grabbed me outside my building."

"You were alone?" He sounded irritated.

"Yes, but LeMonte was close by and stepped in."

"Sis, make sure you're never alone unless you're in a secure place. I'll explain later. Need to go." He disconnected.

Mia felt overcome with fear, but worried more about Andy as she drove to work. *Why are we both in danger?* She had been involved with heists since college graduation ten years earlier. Not once had she worried about her safety when she wasn't actually pulling a job. Andy sometimes had problems, but those problems never rolled to her. Andy and their father, before he got murdered in prison, had always protected her. No one knew she was part of the family. Now something was amiss. Someone either knew or suspected she was involved. *But why would that suddenly put me in danger?* Mia ran through her head everything she had done since their last heist, and nothing came to mind that would lead anyone to her.

Her thoughts moved to the uncut stones Andy had squandered away gambling instead of turning them over to J.D., the guy who had hired him for the job. *Is that the connection? Was Andy being watched? Were we spotted at Sammy's together? Maybe meeting Andy again at Sammy's isn't a good idea.* Mia decided to call him later and arrange for another meeting place.

Arriving at her office building, Mia noticed a man in the shadows near the lobby stairwell. With the prior night's attack prominent on her mind, she stuck her hand in her purse, gripped the handle of her pistol, and went to the elevator. As she pushed the elevator button, she heard heavy footsteps behind her.

"Good morning, Mia."

Recognizing the voice, she sighed and released her hold on the weapon. "Never thought I'd beat you to work."

"Well, I wouldn't say just because you pushed the button first, means you beat me to work," Lewis said. "Unless you think that second is important."

"I do," she said with a smile. "And I intend to continue believing I beat you to work today."

In the elevator, Lewis's eyes dropped to her hands. "Where's the ring?"

"I parted with it. I figured the longer I kept it, the harder that task would be."

"I thought you'd keep it until after the fundraiser."

"No. I became concerned about losing it. Then I'd end up having to pay for a ring I no longer had."

"Then it was a smart move to return it. If you can't enjoy a piece of jewelry, there's no reason to have it."

Mia glanced at Lewis's gold ring with a large black opal. He always wore shirts that required cufflinks. She guessed he had a huge collection of cufflinks that contained various gemstones. Before the prior day's conversation with him, she never noticed his well-crafted jewelry. *How can he afford that?*

Heading down the hallway with Lewis, moving toward their offices, Mia suddenly recalled Oliver's reaction when she asked if he was an only child. "When I returned the ring, Oliver was talking to another customer, and he mentioned a 'sibling.' From what I've read about him, I thought he was an only child. Do you know if he has any siblings?"

"He had a brother that was shot three or four years ago during a robbery at his L.A. store."

"Dead?"

Lewis nodded. "Never made it to the hospital. Oliver still mourns his brother, and I've heard it rumored the murder contributed to his divorce."

"Why?"

"He went through a real down period and ignored his wife, threw himself one-hundred percent into his work, and cut off the rest of the world. Oliver seems to have snapped out of it. Maybe it took the divorce to do that."

"Is the killer behind bars?"

"No. He's still on the loose. I doubt he'll ever be found." Lewis's eyes fixed on Mia's face. "You interested in Oliver?"

"No, but I think he might be interested in becoming Feinstein's client, so it's good to know talking points. Bringing up his family will definitely be off the table for small chit-chat."

"Yeah, that wouldn't endear him to the agency. The boss has been working on bringing LeMonte on board for almost a year. I've been talking up the agency whenever I see him. You doing the same thing could help pull him in."

"Since I gave back the ring, I probably won't have another chance."

"He gets invited to parties, so you might have another opportunity."

"If I get one, I'll take it. I like helping to bring in clients."

Two hours later, Mia sat in the conference room during the BMW presentation. To her surprise, Gunther's attention was clearly focused on it and not on her like last time. When it ended, Mia and Lewis gathered up their folders and notebooks, preparing to leave the room, which was expected by Feinstein. He was highly skilled in signing up clients, and after a presentation was the ideal time. However, he preferred to do it in a private setting with the potential client.

As Mia headed toward the door, Gunther stood and walked to her. "Are you going to be attending the fundraiser tomorrow evening?"

"Yes. Will you be there?"

"I'm a big supporter of Southeast Hospital."

"Then I'll see you tomorrow evening." Mia forced a smile. Running into Gunther at the event wasn't anything she would look forward to.

Outside the conference room, Lewis said, "Gunther was elected to their board about six months ago."

Oh, great. "Will he be seated at one of Feinstein's

tables?"

"No. Board members have their own tables."

Mia walked in the hallway next to Lewis. "You did a great job on the presentation."

"Thanks. That's the first time I've made it all the way through without fumbling. I guess, after seven years, I'm finally starting to get the hang of the job."

When Mia stepped into her office, she saw a message slip on her desk. LeMonte had called, requesting her to return his call. Staring at the message, Mia recalled he never asked for her phone number. She had no intention of returning his call until after she had spoken with Andy to find out what additional information, if any, he wanted her to obtain from LeMonte.

Thinking about Andy, she took the burner phone out and headed to the lobby to call him.

"Something wrong, Sis?" he asked the minute he answered.

"I'm getting bad vibes about meeting you at Sammy's again. I don't know for sure I was followed after leaving there on Tuesday night, but I don't want to chance it."

"Got it. We'll meet at a friend's apartment. The friend works until midnight. And you can approach without being seen."

"How's that?"

"Go to a bar called *Frank's Place*. It's a real dive, not as classy as Sammy's."

Mia wasn't sure if Andy was joking about Sammy's being classy or if he was serious. If it was the latter, she thought her brother didn't get out enough.

Andy continued. "It's on the same street as Sammy's but a few blocks east. Walk straight through the place to the restrooms. Near them is the back door. It's never locked and doesn't have an alarm on it. Go out that door and go to the apartment building next door. No fence separates the buildings. Walk in the back door and take the stairwell to the second floor. The apartment is on the right. Most tenants use the side door by the parking lot and the stairwell by it. I've never run into anyone on the back stairwell."

"Apartment number?"

"218. Have a Uber or taxi drop you right in front of the bar. Don't walk there."

"Okay. See you later."

Mia kept busy the rest of the day, working with Lewis on laying out material for a series of television commercials for a client who owned a line of cosmetics.

When she returned to her office to drop off folders and collect her purse to go home, the message light flashed on her desk phone. Mia tapped a button on it and listened to three messages. One came from a client and two from LeMonte. She returned only the client's call.

Chapter 6

Mia followed Andy's directions and arrived at Apartment 218. As she stepped through the doorway, she glanced at the décor—frilly curtains, a flower-patterned upholstered couch with a matching chair, a picture of a cute blonde with her brother prominently displayed on an end table—and the place was spotless. "Is this Maxine's apartment?"

"Yep." Andy moved to the fridge. "Want a beer?"

"Sure."

As they sat at the table and drank, Andy asked, "Think you were followed from the office?"

"I kept checking, but I didn't spot any cars tailing me."

Andy grabbed Mia's hand. "What happened to the ring?"

"He made a pass, so I gave it back."

Andy's eyes narrowed. "You already broke up with him? We still need him."

"We only had one date. That isn't much of a relationship to call it a break up, and I didn't tell him to get lost. He called me a few times today, wanting me to call him."

"Did you?"

"Nope. I wanted to know where the job stood first. I had dinner at his house, and he gave me a tour. There are surveillance cameras everywhere and a laser security system in the dining room. There aren't any surveillance cameras upstairs, but one on the main floor points to the stairwell. At least one guard roamed around the outside of the house. When I went to the bathroom, I accidentally opened a door across the hall, a door LeMonte didn't open on the tour. It led to a basement. There was a light on downstairs."

"Good job, Sis. How about windows in the dining room?"

"There aren't any, but there's a fireplace." A crooked smile crossed her face. "You could play Santa Claus."

He tapped his chin. "I'll have to think about that." Andy took a notepad and pen off of the counter. "Draw me the floor plan."

Mia sketched it out, labeling rooms, and the door going to the basement. "The room dimensions are a little out of whack, and this square off the kitchen is servant's quarters. There could be an additional problem since this house is owned by LeMonte and his family."

"Family?"

"Yes. Three cousins, an aunt, and uncle. They all stay there when they're in New York. Since you heard his ex-wife took him to the cleaners, the family ownership thing is probably why she never got the house in the divorce. Who knows? Maybe all of his places are family-owned."

"Are any of them going to be showing up in the next few days?"

"LeMonte hasn't heard, but they don't inform him of their visits in advance, and all family members have their own bedrooms." Mia put down the pen. "Did you learn anything from Dad's buddy about who might be snooping around?"

"Yeah. Not good. He's gotten wind that someone is searching for Dad's loot."

"What makes him think that?"

"He seemed a little reluctant to give details, maybe because it's one of his buddies. And, first time ever, he asked if I had a sister."

Mia's hands turned cold. "What did you say?"

"Nope, but someone must suspect. When I asked if he knew about the heist at LeMonte's, he just shrugged. Then I asked about our new employer, just to see what he had to say about the guy, but he wouldn't talk about him. I got strange vibes from Dad's buddy. Something's up. He might not be reliable anymore. He and Dad go way back, but Dad's gone and loyalties evaporate once you're dead and buried. Maybe that's what got him killed in the joint. I sure wish I could talk to Dad. All we can do is guess. I'm not sure I can trust the new boss."

"What does that mean? You don't think he'll take care of your problem with J.D. once you turn over the diamonds?"

"That's how I see it."

Mia rubbed her forehead. "From the beginning of this job, I thought you were set up—the guy that won those diamonds you gambled is the same guy that wants you to steal LeMonte's uncut stones. Maybe he hoped you couldn't get to them, and you'd tap into Dad's stash to get out of trouble. What do you think?"

"The guy's been in the business for a long time. Dad even partnered with him on a few jobs. Everyone that ever worked with Dad probably knows about the stash. But we have no idea where it is, so following us is pointless."

"But the guy wouldn't know that."

"Good point."

"You still have to replace those diamonds or hand over five million in cash. So what's the game plan?"

"Saturday night. You've already been to LeMonte's house. Get invited back, but this time insist on driving yourself."

Mia smiled. "An intruder will be in my trunk and the laser alarm system won't be activated, but you'll still have to deal with the security guards and the surveillance cameras."

"Those I can handle. The only problem will be if he's moved the diamonds to the store. I've been studying the new security system he installed there. If the stones aren't in his home safe, we'll work on that Sunday night. And if that all fails, I do have a last resort possibility, but that'll be cash, not diamonds."

"What?"

"Don't want to talk about it yet."

Mia wondered what that was all about and then switched to the upcoming job. "Getting back to LeMonte's house. What if other family members are there?"

"Text me as soon as you discover that, and give me as much info as possible. That doesn't mean it won't still be a go. It just means I need to be on the lookout. And I don't intend to make a move before 9:30. Where in the house would he be entertaining you at that hour?"

"The dining room is at the front of the house, across the hall from the front parlor. I'll make sure he entertains me either in the back parlor, or in his..." she gave her brother a mischievous smile, "...bedroom."

"Make it the back parlor. He might turn on the laser system before he goes upstairs."

"He didn't last time."

"You okay with spending time in his bedroom?"

"Not a problem. But he could already have an engagement for Saturday night, which will blow the whole plan."

"He called you several times today. He'll break an engagement for you."

"Okay. I'll return his call when I get home and line it up. Since you don't trust the new employer, are you going to deal directly with J.D.?"

"Yep. I'll give him the diamonds he's owed. After that problem's resolved and my butt isn't on the line, I'll contact the new guy and negotiate. See if I can't get enough dough for the rest of the diamonds to pay off the shop mortgage and a substantial fee for my assistant." Andy winked at his sister.

Mia's brow rose. "Good plan. Anything else?"

"Nope, that's it. I'll call you Saturday afternoon to tell you where to pick me up."

Mia hugged her brother goodbye and left the apartment. She reversed the route she had taken earlier to see him. Waiting in the bar to exit until her Uber arrived, she saw a black BMW on the other side of the street. A man wearing a blue Yankee's cap sat in the driver's seat.

As her Uber pulled away from the curb, so did the black BMW. She moved her eyes back and forth between the side mirrors, trying to see if the car made a U-turn. With all the cars on the road, it quickly vanished from her sight. After traveling a few blocks, a black BMW pulled out of a side street and drove two cars behind her. Mia saw the car each time she checked the Uber's mirrors, but when she reached her building, it was nowhere in sight.

After entering her unit, Mia changed. She couldn't get through to her company voice mail to locate LeMonte's number. *Damn! I won't be able to reach him until tomorrow*

As she went to the fridge for a soda, a peep came from her phone, signaling a new text message. Mia took a swig of her drink, tapped on the message icon, and saw it came from "unidentified caller." It read: "I like the maroon dress you wore today. It nicely shows off your curves."

Since she hadn't been home long, Mia wondered if the "unidentified caller" was the guy who had tailed her. *Could he be watching my apartment?* She went to the front window, peered out through an opening at the edge of her blinds, and scanned the street below for a black BMW. She spotted two but couldn't see if anyone was in either vehicle. Then she saw a man, wearing a blue Yankee's cap, standing near a light post. A chill washed over her. She had hoped it was just her imagination that she was being followed, but now that hope evaporated. Someone was definitely onto her. Mia wasn't sure if it was because she was Leo Carlyle's daughter and might know of his stash or if it was because of the jobs she had done with her brother. Sinking down in a chair, she worried it might be both, which meant Andy was also being watched. If he spotted a tail, Mia feared Andy's hot temper would kick in and things would go from bad to worse.

Chapter 7

When Mia strolled into the agency, Lorraine, the company receptionist, hurried toward her. "Hey, Mia, are you taking a date to the fundraiser?"

"No."

"Are you driving or taking a cab?"

"I'm driving."

"Can I bum a ride?"

"Sure. I could pick you up at six thirty. Will that work?"

"Yeah. I'll wait for you in front of my building. Oh, Dawson's coming in today."

"Thanks for the warning."

"I'm sure he'll brighten our day." Lorraine laughed and went back to her desk.

Nigel Dawson was Feinstein's elusive partner, the money man who helped establish the agency fifteen years earlier. He was short, heavyset, and approaching sixty with a recessed hairline. Expensive Armani suits hung on his squatty frame. Dawson's name was on the company logo, stationery, and checks. He had an office with his name prominently displayed on the door, but he only showed up at the agency a few times a year and never went to company parties. Mia doubted he understood the business or anything they did. On his rare visits, he snacked on chips as he wandered around, leaving a trail of crumbs while he chatted with every employee longer than anyone would have liked. Sometimes he'd flop down in a chair in Mia's office, and she'd have to make small talk until he decided to move on.

Feinstein ran the agency and was responsible for its growth. Still, since Dawson was a partner, he was treated with respect and like he had some knowledge of the business. All employees dreaded the few times he showed up.

Even though Mia felt the same way, Dawson had played a small hand in her getting a job at Feinstein & Dawson. Prior to joining the ad agency, she worked for a company that designed billboard advertising. Dawson came in one day to see her boss. On his way out the door, he stopped at the table where she was designing a billboard campaign. He mentioned that there was an opening at Feinstein & Dawson and gave her his card. When she saw he was the Dawson in Feinstein & Dawson, she applied for the position. Had it not been for him, she wouldn't have known about the opening.

Still, she hoped she'd be in a presentation when he made his rounds. Mia eased down in her chair and glanced at her watch—8:38 a.m. She wanted to have the conversation with LeMonte before Dawson dropped by her office. *His store probably opens at 10:00 a.m.* Mia wrote down the number he had left. While she waited to call, Mia dug into the project files on her desk.

Mia was so absorbed in her work she didn't notice Lewis entering her office. "Mia," he said, and she jumped. "Didn't mean to startle you. I should have knocked before I walked in."

"No problem."

"You mentioned you weren't taking anyone to the fundraiser. Would you consider going with me?"

"Can't. I'm picking up Lorraine."

"Oh." Disappointment was evident on Lewis's face.

"But I'd be happy to go with you to lunch today if you're free."

Lewis smiled. "I've got a client meeting. Have you got plans for the weekend?"

Mia nodded, hoping she would have plans. "How about lunch Monday?"

"We're on."

"Is Mr. Dawson in the office?"

"No. His first stop was visiting me. Hung around my office for over thirty minutes. He had intended to be here most of the day, but he received a call and took off." Lewis smiled. "We probably won't be seeing him again for three or four months."

"Glad you had the privilege of entertaining him."

"You missed your chance. When he was in my office, he said you were next on his list."

After Lewis walked out, Mia's eyes moved to the clock on the wall—11:05 a.m. She closed the door and then placed the call to LeMonte. It went straight to voice mail. Mia left a message.

As she waited for his call, she found it impossible to concentrate on her projects and kept glancing at the clock. Shortly after two, she stood and stretched, and then headed to the cafeteria for a sandwich.

It was almost 4:30 p.m. when LeMonte called.

"Hello." She tried not to sound anxious.

"Hello, Mia. I'm glad you returned my call. Sorry I didn't get back to you earlier. I've been tied up in meetings. I called to see if you would be interested in going out with me again or if I had completely blown that chance."

"I probably overreacted, and thank you again for stepping in when the stranger grabbed me near my apartment."

"Must admit it didn't look like you really needed my help. You flipped that guy flat on his back."

"Well, I've taken some self-defense classes. That was the first time that training paid off."

"Are you free tomorrow evening?"

"Yes, I am."

"Would you care to have dinner with me?"

"Yes. But since you mentioned you always run into people at restaurants who want to catch up, I don't mind having dinner at your home again. I'm sorry...That sounds so forward, doesn't it? I don't want to give you the wrong impression."

"I wanted to ask you how you would feel about having dinner there again, but I didn't want you to change your mind about seeing me. Can I pick you up at 7:30?"

"Oliver, I plan on spending most of the day tomorrow with my aunt. Would it be okay if I drove to your place?"

"So you can make a quick getaway if things get out of hand?"

"No, that's not it. It would just be easier to go from my aunt's apartment to your place."

"I could pick you up there?"

"I'll have my car. Maybe we should plan on having dinner another night."

"No. If you wish to drive yourself, that won't be a problem." He proceeded to give Mia directions to his house.

"Thanks. I didn't pay attention to where we were going when you drove."

"When you reach the gate, push the button on the stand, and I'll open it for you."

After they hung up, Mia sighed. *He seemed to resist letting me drive. Why? Maybe he really is worried that I'll take off if he gets too friendly.*

On her way home from work, she didn't spot any cars following her cab. She began to feel a sense of relief, but then an unpleasant thought snapped into her mind. *Did Andy see someone tailing him? If so, was that someone still around to talk about it?*

Mia mulled over her concerns while she dressed for the evening's event. She toyed with taking a small clutch purse but decided against it since her pistol couldn't fit. Even though she hadn't been followed to her apartment, that didn't mean it wouldn't happen again. And if Andy had taken care of one guy, that might spur on more that needed to be dealt with. With that thought, Mia stuffed a few more things into her oversized purse.

* * *

Lorraine was waiting outside her building when Mia stopped at the curb. "Hi." She scooted into the passenger seat. "Did you hear about Gunther?"

"What about him?" Mia cut into traffic.

"He might lose his Mercedes franchise."

"Why?"

"Now this is strictly hush hush. I shouldn't even know about it." Lorraine stared at Mia.

"Okay. I won't blab about it."

"From what I overheard, he has a partner…a silent partner. No one mentioned the name, so I can't fill you in on that. But the partner loaned Gunther a bunch of money. Don't know how much, and I guess Gunther secured the loan with his interest in the franchise. Anyway, Gunther hasn't been paying the partner. Goodbye franchise."

"You said he might lose it, so it's not a done deal?" Mia asked as she thought that would explain why he wanted the presentation changed from a Mercedes to a BMW.

"It kind of sounded like it was close to a done deal, but I can't be sure. Didn't catch the end of the conversation."

Lorraine was a cute blonde, had a bubbly personality, and clients liked her, but she loved to gossip and eavesdrop on conversations. Mia knew from past experience to check if Lorraine was close by before she had a private conversation with anyone in the office.

"Hey, you thinking about dating Lewis?"

"No. Why?"

"I heard you were going to lunch with him on Monday."

"We're going to lunch as colleagues, nothing more."

"Boy, that isn't the way I heard it."

"Then you heard wrong." Mia pulled into a parking stall at the Marriott Hotel.

Lorraine raised her eyebrows. "We'll see."

When they reached the room reserved for the fundraiser, Mia and Lorraine were each given a name tag. Mia looked for tables reserved for Feinstein's agency while Lorraine went to the bar.

Stopping at one of Feinstein's tables, Mia saw napkins and other items had already been placed on over half of the chairs. She picked a table with only two unclaimed chairs, pulled a sweater out of her purse, and laid it across those chairs. In spite of Lorraine's proclivity to gossiping, Mia enjoyed her company and didn't want to end up sitting between people with dates or guys who had hit on her.

"Got you this," Lorraine said, handing Mia a glass of white wine. "I was starting to think there wouldn't be any good-looking, single guys showing up, but guess who just walked in?"

Mia followed Lorraine's gaze to the entrance doorway and saw LeMonte."

"Oliver LeMonte." She turned to Lorraine. "How do you know him?"

"Oliver LeMonte? Is he here too?"

"He's the tall guy with brown hair, talking to Feinstein."

"That's not Oliver LeMonte. That's his cousin, Vince…Vince Tolbert."

"Are you sure?" Mia tried to inconspicuously glance at him.

"Yeah. Isn't he dreamy? I met him and his cousin, Oliver, at Feinstein's spring party. They didn't stay long. That was a bummer. Maybe Feinstein will invite him to sit at one of his tables. What do you think?"

"Possibly." Mia stared at the man, wondering why he had lied to her and claimed to be Oliver LeMonte.

"Is he Oliver's partner?"

"No. He's a private investigator."

Mia felt her mouth drop open. *Private investigator?*

"Doesn't that seem so much more exciting than a jeweler? Moving between thugs, thieves, criminals. Working in the dark underground, investigating crimes. Probably stuff the police couldn't solve. I wonder if he's packing, ready to pull out his pistol and bring down a criminal. Thrilling, huh? Hope he sits by us."

Mia's stomach churned as she heard Lorraine's description of the man's job. Hunting down criminals was a dangerous job, but being a criminal was even more dangerous. Even sitting by him suddenly became a risky proposition. To calm her nerves, Mia inhaled and exhaled slowly a few times.

"You okay?" Lorraine asked.

"Yeah. Why?"

"You look a little pale."

Mia forced a smile. "I just need more wine." She downed the remainder in her glass. "Do you want me to get you another one?"

"Sure. I'm going to go and talk to Vince."

Mia headed to the bar, wondering how much Vince knew about her. *Is there any possibility he only suspects I'm involved with crimes but doesn't know for sure? Before I met the investigator, Andy checked out LeMonte's store safe but didn't rob it. Maybe, somehow, he discovered Andy had been there and tailed him, hoping to track down the stolen goods. Andy met me in the park. Could that have caused his interest in me?* More questions kept springing into Mia's head as she sipped on another glass of wine.

Since Mia thought there was a slight chance that Vince hadn't put all the pieces together, she decided to try and play it cool and not let him rattle her. Talking to Andy about the new problem that just surfaced was on top of her to-do list when she got home.

As Mia set down a glass of wine on the table for Lorraine, she heard Lorraine call out, "Oh, Mia."

Mia turned around and saw Lorraine approaching with Vince.

"Let me introduce you to Vince Tolbert. Vince this is Mia Sloan. She also works for Feinstein & Dawson."

"Happy to meet you, Mia," Vince said, stretching out his hand and not giving any indication that he already knew her.

"It's a pleasure to meet you, Mr. Tolbert." Mia shook his hand.

"Please call me Vince."

"Certainly, Vince."

Lorraine's face glowed with excitement. "Vince is going to sit with us."

"I reserved the last two chairs at this table. You two sit here." Mia picked up her sweater. "I'll find a place at another one of Mr. Feinstein's tables." Out of the corner of her eye, she saw Gunther heading her way. She looped around the table to avoid him.

"Mia, I saved you and Lorraine seats right here," Lewis said, standing behind a chair.

Thinking she'd rather be seated by Lewis than Gunther, she went to him. "Thanks." She put her sweater over the back of the chair. "Lorraine won't be joining us. She's going to sit at that table with Vince Tolbert." Mia nodded in that direction.

"I'm sure Lorraine can keep him entertained," Lewis said with a pleased expression on his face.

"Vince is Oliver LeMonte's cousin."

Gunther stepped next to her. "Mia, I'm so glad you were able to make it. Would you care to sit at my table?"

She noticed Lewis glaring at Gunther. "Thank you, Hank, but Mr. Feinstein expects me to sit at one of his tables."

"How about having a drink with me in the lounge after dinner?"

"Sorry, I took another employee to this event and promised I'd drive her home."

"I'd be happy to have her join us, too."

"I'll ask her after dinner and let you know."

A tapping sound came from the podium, signaling it was time for participants to take their seats. After a few minutes of commotion, everyone was seated and talking had died down.

"Thank you, ladies and gentlemen, for attending Southeast Hospital's annual fundraiser event," said the hospital's executive director. "After dinner, there will be a short program. Bon appétit."

Mia was in the middle of eating the main course when she heard a soft chime sound coming from her purse.

Lewis glanced at her purse along with the woman, a co-worker's date, sitting on the other side. Irritated that she hadn't put her cell phones on vibrate, she said, "Sorry." She rummaged through her purse and discovered the sound came from her burner phone. A text. Guessing it was important, she held her phone in her purse to prevent those sitting near her from seeing the message and tapped on it. It read: "RUN, MIA, RUN. Meet you at our place."

Chapter 8

Fear shot through her body. Andy and Mia had often talked about this possibility. Swallowing hard, she had no idea what had happened but knew she had to keep her wits if she hoped to survive. She glanced around and saw a few women heading out of the room and assumed they were going to the restroom.

Mia looked at Lewis. "Excuse me. I'll be right back. And if the server comes around, please have her take my plate."

"Sure."

In order not to draw any unwanted attention, Mia left her sweater on the back of the chair and made her way out of the room. She entered the restroom, went into a stall, and pulled her regular cell phone out of her purse. After dismantling it, Mia wrapped the SIM card in toilet paper and discarded it in the stall's garbage container. Gripping the remaining pieces in her hand, she left the restroom and dropped the disassembled phone in a trash container by the hotel's side entrance.

A taxi-for-hire stood by the curb. Mia jumped in and gave him the address of the nearest department store.

As he drove, Mia's eyes searched for a tail. She couldn't spot anyone following them but feared an ambush.

The driver stopped on the curb in a red zone in front of the department store. Mia paid him and headed straight to the women's department, picked out a pair of jeans and a sweat shirt, and went into a dressing room. She slipped on the new outfit and pulled a blonde, curly wig out of her purse. Earlier, she'd intended to use it to elude a tail. She stuffed her blouse and skirt into her purse and walked to the cash register.

"I'd like to wear these. Can you cut the tags and ring me up, please?"

The sales clerk nodded, removed the tags, and rang up the total price.

Mia paid cash, took the escalator to the main floor, slipped on a pair of glasses, and then walked to the bus stop half a block away. While she waited for the bus, she cautiously scanned the area.

Within fifteen minutes, she was seated on the bus and headed toward her next destination about five miles away. Each time the bus stopped, she checked out each new passenger that entered.

Reaching her stop, she felt relieved when she was the only one that got off. From there, she walked to the Universal Gym, a place she had gone to once. On that one and only visit, she joined as a V.I.P. member, using a fictitious name, and rented a locker. She paid her membership and rental fee annually with money orders. She pulled her membership card out of a hidden compartment in her purse and showed it to a man with bulging muscles, standing at the front counter.

His eyes roved over her body, and then he looked at the card. "Cindy, do you come here often?"

"I used to come all the time but changed jobs, so it's been a while."

He leaned over the counter. "Think you can make it more often?"

"I'm hoping."

Three women walked in.

He handed her back her card as his attention diverted to the women.

Mia went through the door next to the counter and walked to the locker room. She retrieved a duffle bag from her locker, stepped into a dressing stall and closed the curtain. To make sure nothing was missing, she checked the contents—clothing, shoes, wig, a knife in a sheath, and a wad of money. Then she flipped off her heels, pulled out a dark blue jogging suit and athletic shoes, and changed. Next, she strapped the knife to her calf and hid it under her pants. She took out the light, tawny-brown wig with a blunt cut which hit below Mia's ears and bangs hitting just above her eyes. She threw everything in the duffle bag.

Mia left the stall and checked herself in the mirror and then applied heavy, dark makeup around her eyes and bright red lipstick. Satisfied that she wouldn't be easily recognized, she exited and had no trouble flagging a taxi. She looked at her watch—11:23 p.m.

"Where to, lady?" asked the bearded, stocky driver.

"Grand Central Station."

As he pulled away from the curb, it suddenly

dawned on her that she might not be able to catch a train to her destination at that hour. "Would it be possible for you to drive me to a place not far from New Haven?"

"New Haven, Connecticut?"

"Yes."

"I can do that, but it's going to go cost you."

"Would five hundred be enough?"

"Yeah, that would work. But I need it in advance."

Mia handed him the money. She leaned back in the seat and closed her eyes. Aunt Thelma's farm—their "place"—was where she and Andy were raised. Her aunt, a hard working woman, took in Mia's mother, three-year-old Andy, and infant Mia when their mother left their father. Mia was halfway through elementary school before she learned that Aunt Thelma wasn't a relative. Mia and Andy loved Aunt Thelma, and the woman always referred to them as her nephew and niece. She couldn't have had a better childhood than growing up on a farm. Then everything changed when Mia was sixteen—her mother became ill and died, and her father re-entered their lives.

Ten years later, Andy and Mia inherited the farm when Thelma passed. To keep it a safe, secure place, they decided not to have the title transferred to their names. Thelma remained the owner of record. Andy hired Brent Rye, a middle-aged man who was a dear friend of Thelma's, to manage the place, keep it maintained, pay utilities, taxes, and insurance. An account had been set up to pay him. Andy handled it for a few months, and after Mia started working for Feinstein, she took over replenishing funds whenever needed.

She thought about Andy. *Is he safe and already at the farm?* She was aware he also had several escape routes. Still, she worried about J.D., a gangster she had never met, and wondered if he had moved up the timetable to collect Andy's debt or if the new employer, the guy Andy didn't trust, was behind the need for a quick departure.

Then her mind wandered to Vince Tolbert. When she met him at LeMonte's Fine Jewelry, he acted like he was in charge. There was nothing that indicated he wasn't the boss. He lent her a ring and appeared to be interested in her. He even made a serious pass at her at his house. *Was it all a pretense to help him solve a crime?* Pretense was a ploy she had often used to set up a crime. Still, she felt irritated about being used. Mia couldn't deny her immediate attraction to him the first time she saw him in the jewelry store. *Will I ever see him again? Or will Andy and I have to keep running?*

"Lady, we're close to New Haven. I'll need some directions."

Mia sat up straight and gave the driver directions to the spot where she wanted to be dropped off, which was about a mile from the farm. She didn't want anyone, except Andy, to know her destination, not even the taxi driver.

Stopping at the edge of a deserted road, the driver asked, "I don't see any houses around here. Are you sure you want me to let you out here?"

"Yes."

The driver gave Mia a puzzled look as she climbed out of the car with her duffle bag.

She stood on the shoulder of the road and watched the driver make a u-turn to get back to the interstate. Then Mia walked to the next intersection, turned right, and headed to the next country road about a half a mile away. There, she turned left and proceeded to the lane that went to the farm. Not one vehicle drove by her, which was what she expected in the dark, wee hours of the morning.

Seeing the pitch-black dirt lane, Mia set down her duffle bag, unzipped it, and rummaged through her purse and retrieved a penlight. She turned it on, swung the strap of her duffle bag over her shoulder, and made her way to the farm house. After she unlocked the door, she only opened it slightly, thinking there was a chance Andy could be inside sleeping. Guessing he'd have a pistol near him, she didn't want to startle him.

"Andy, it's me," Mia yelled through the small opening. Intensely listening for any sound coming from inside the house, she waited on the porch. A few minutes later, she yelled again, "Andy, it's Mia." She waited again. Not hearing a peep inside the house, she opened the door wider and flipped on the light switch on the other side of the door frame.

Mia stepped inside and looked around. Except for thick layer of dust on everything and a few cobwebs in the corners, everything looked exactly the way it had six years prior, her last time at the farm.

Wearily, she climbed stairs to the bedrooms and decided she'd sleep in one of the bedrooms near the front, thinking she could hear Andy entering the house better from there. She picked the bedroom her mother had once occupied and made up the bed.

Mia knew Andy had been in tight spots before. He had sometimes gone to the farm while he sorted things out but always managed to work out problems. Feeling confident her brother would be there soon,

Mia climbed in bed, closed her eyes, and drifted off.

Chapter 9

As light filled the bedroom, Mia awoke with a start. Confused and disoriented, she looked around the room, and then her flight to her Aunt's farm flooded into her mind. The light in the room flickered. She glanced at her watch on the nightstand—3:37 a.m. Hearing a car engine outside, she assumed Andy had finally arrived, so she hurried to the window. A black sedan moved down the lane. Andy always drove trucks, but Mia figured he switched vehicles in order to get out of the city. The car stopped near the porch. She frowned. Andy always parked behind the house.

Two men stepped out of the vehicle. One wore a gun strapped over his shoulder.

A chill swept through Mia's body. Trembling, she slipped on her jogging suit and shoes, and tucked her pistol in the waistband. As she crept down the stairs, someone pounded on the door. Through the shear front curtains, she saw another set of headlights pulling down the lane.

Aware of several places she could hide undetected

in the barn, Mia stealthily moved to the back door as pounding on the front door continued. She slowly unlocked the door. Before opening it, she peered out a window and scanned the area behind the house. Not seeing anyone, she opened the door and edged out onto the back porch, closing the door behind her. Hurrying to the closest tree, Mia scooted behind it. After surveying the yard again, she began to run toward the barn. On her way, she leapt over a pile of dirt.

Instead of clearing it, she tumbled into a four foot hole. Trying to regain her bearings and hurting from her fall, she sat up. As she wiped the loose dirt from her face, to her horror, the beam of a flashlight shined on her.

"Are you okay, Miss Sloan?" said a familiar voice.

"No, I'm not, Vince. And what are you doing here?" Mia's eyes darted between Vince and the armed man standing next to him.

"Well, I haven't come to have you arrested if you're worried about that."

Holding onto her sore side, Mia slowly rose to her feet. "Why would I be concerned about that? I'm a law abiding citizen."

"If you're a law abiding citizen, then why did you run when someone knocked on your door?"

"Because I'm here alone, it's after three a.m., and there have been house invasions around here."

"Can I help you get out of the hole?" He stretched a hand toward her.

"Certainly not. I can manage quite well without any assistance." Mia placed her hands on the flat ground above the hole and attempted to pull herself up. The pain in her side intensified, and she sank down.

Vince slid down into the hole beside her. "Where does it hurt?"

"Why are you here?" Mia asked again, leaning against the side of the hole.

"To protect you."

"And what makes you think I need your protection?"

"Let me help you get out of the hole first, and then we can discuss it." He took her hand. "Can you tell me where you are injured?"

Mia didn't want Vince to think she couldn't manage on her own, but she doubted she could crawl out without a little help. Gesturing toward the armed man, she said, "If your friend up there could give me a hand, I'm sure I can get out."

"Owen, you heard the lady," Vince said to the guy.

Mia rose to her feet while pain rippled through her side. She reached out and grabbed Owen's hands. He pulled her out of the hole while Vince lifted her legs.

Clutching her side just above the handle of her pistol, Mia trudged to the house as Vince climbed out of the hole.

He quickly caught up to her and gripped her elbow. "Mia, it's obvious you're in pain. Put your arm around my neck, and I'll carry you into the house."

"Vince," she said through gritted teeth, trying not show any pain "...or are you Oliver now?"

"My name is Vince. I didn't want to lie to you. I'll explain everything in the house."

Mia continued shuffling toward the house. "I don't want to talk to you. I'd like you to leave. If you're under some misguided belief that I need your protection, sit in your car out front."

Vince suddenly swooped her up into his arms. "You're injured, and I intend to find out how badly."

With the pain in her side, Mia didn't have the energy to fight him off and kept her hand on her sore side as he carried her into the house.

Vince gently laid her on the sofa. "I'm going to unzip your top. This is strictly for medical purposes, nothing more. Understand?"

"I can do that." Mia unzipped the top of her jogging suit. The instant it was down, she felt him touching her bare skin.

"This could be part of the problem." Vince pulled her pistol out of her waistband and set it on the coffee table. "You're black-and-blue all around where the handle was pressing into you." He began moving his hand over her ribs.

Mia flinched. "Ouch."

"Can you breathe okay?"

"Uh-huh."

"Owen, get Walt."

Owen went out the front door.

Vince moved his hand over Mia's stomach. "Any pain here?"

"No."

A short, lean man, carrying a medical bag, walked through the door with Owen.

"Do you always bring a doctor with you when you make late-night calls?"

"I wouldn't call this late night...more like early morning. Walt isn't a doctor. He was a medic in the army. Besides his medical expertise, he's highly skilled with all types of electronics." Vince turned to Walt. "I think her bottom two ribs are cracked. Can you check to make sure they're not broken?"

Walt took Vince's place, opened his medical bag, and slipped on a pair of latex gloves.

As Walt ran his fingers over them, Mia bit her bottom lip but didn't make a sound.

"They're not broken," Walt said to Vince. "The handle of her gun smashed into them when she fell. If she begins to have any trouble breathing, she should be taken to the local hospital." Walt turned to Mia. "Would you like a couple of pain pills?"

Mia nodded.

Walt pulled a container from his bag and took out two pills. "They should take care of the pain for four to six hours. I'll leave this container on the kitchen counter if you should need more."

Vince handed her a glass of water.

She swallowed the pills with a sip of water. As Walt gathered up his supplies, Mia said, "Thanks."

"You're welcome, Miss Sloan."

"Please, call me Mia."

Walt smiled at her and then turned his attention to Vince. "I'll be in the van if you need me."

"Have you picked up any chatter?"

"No. It's been pretty quiet."

"Probably will be for a while."

Walt left with Owen.

"Chatter about what?" Mia asked.

"The equipment in the van picks up all noise within a mile radius. Animal sounds have been filtered out, and other noises are also filtered out once determined they're harmless."

"What are you looking for?"

"Unwelcome visitors."

"Well, go look in the mirror. Then you'll have one nabbed."

Vince sank down into the chair next to her. "Mia, I know you're angry, but I really am here to help you, not to harm you."

"You said outside you'd explain. Start explaining."

He went to hold Mia's hand. She immediately withdrew it.

"Okay," he said, "I've been searching for the man responsible for my cousin's death—Oliver's brother. He was killed three years ago during a robbery in L.A. A couple of months ago, I got wind that the culprit was in New York and planning to steal a shipment of uncut diamonds."

"How did you get wind of that?"

"My sources will remain anonymous. I wasn't informed who was going to be robbed or when it was going to take place. As you know, a heist did occur about four weeks ago."

"And how would I know that?"

His brow rose. "You are very good at this, aren't you?"

"Good at what?"

"Playing the innocent role. And I must admit, I never would've suspected the gorgeous woman with the dazzling smile I saw at Feinstein's party, who had worked for him for six years, was a skilled thief."

"Before you start making wild accusations, you better have proof."

"Don't have proof of you in the act, but I have recordings."

"Recordings?"

"Yes. From when you met your brother in the park before you paid me a visit at the jewelry store and the night you saw him in Maxine Stewart's apartment."

Mia stared at him, wondering how long she'd been on his radar. Then her thoughts drifted to Andy. She needed to warn him to stay away from the farm. It was no longer a safe place. "What is it you want?" she snapped.

Vince raised his hand in a stop motion. "Calm down, Mia. I don't intend to turn over the recordings to any law enforcement agency. Let me finish explaining, and then you can ask me all the questions you want. Okay?"

Mia nodded.

"A source told me Andy Carlyle, your brother, was involved in the heist. At that point, I thought he might be the person responsible for my cousin's death. I put a 24/7 surveillance on him and soon learned he and an associate were hired to do the job. But instead of turning over all of the stolen diamonds, he gambled away part of them. To make up the shortage, he planned another heist. I didn't know LeMonte's Fine Jewelry was the target until he broke into the store on Monday night and cracked the safe. Oliver had purchased some uncut diamonds, but they weren't being stored in that safe. Your brother didn't take anything that night. The following day, additional security equipment was installed, which I told you about when you stopped by after talking to your brother in the park. Even though nothing was missing, I mentioned the store had been robbed to see how that information would play out.

"A couple of days ago, Andy visited Brayton Kirby."

That was a name Mia had never heard. Since Andy was going to see one of their father's long-time buddies, she guessed that was him.

Vince went on. "Kirby wouldn't talk to me without a payment of twenty grand up front. He gave no hint what he had to offer, but I had no intention of walking away from an opportunity that might have a bearing on locating Ethan's—my cousin—killer. When you tried to reach me on Friday, I was obtaining the cash and spending time with Kirby.

"He told me that Andy and his sister are in serious trouble. The details were sketchy. No names. But it is either someone you have done a job for or someone you are planning to do a job for. Whoever that someone is knows Andy and his sister. Kirby gave me the impression that he knew you existed but not your identity. He also said that person was behind Ethan's death. The $20,000 was well spent." Vince attempted to take Mia's hand again, but again she moved it out of his reach. "Mia, the way I look at it, we're on the same side."

"Same side? Are you planning to help Andy and me steal LeMonte's diamonds?"

Vince's eyes sagged. "You don't know?"

"Know what?"

"From the way you took off at the fundraiser, I assumed…"

Mia interrupted. "I thought I did a good job getting away from there. How did you track me?"

"When you were at my house, I put a bug on your purse. It was a good thing you took the same purse to the fundraiser. Otherwise, it would've been a more difficult task, especially since you kept changing your appearance."

The thought of searching for a bug after leaving a jeweler's home never entered Mia's mind. From all the attention he showed her that night, she didn't have the slightest clue he was on to her. "Okay, what is it that I don't know?"

"Andy," he said slowly, his eyes fixed on her face.

"Did you and your men snatch Andy when he pulled into the lane?"

"No."

"Then where is he?"

A sad expression flashed on his face. "Andy's truck was blown up."

"Are you saying...?" she began as her eyes filled with tears. "No...No... No, you're wrong." She choked back a sob. "Andy... Andy...probably wasn't in the truck."

Vince wrapped his arms around her. "Andrew Carlyle was in the truck. That's been confirmed. Mia, I'm so sorry. I thought that was why you took off."

With trembling lips, she stuttered. "He t-t-texted me to run."

"Mia, that's not possible. The explosion occurred before the fundraiser. I knew you and Andy were in trouble, but until the explosion, I didn't realize that would be the outcome. Had that not happened, I never would've showed up at the fundraiser. I had already intended to tell you my true identity, but not that way. I only went to the fundraiser to look after you. Since you appeared to be enjoying yourself when I arrived, I didn't think you had heard. Then during dinner, you looked at your phone and took off."

Tears streamed down Mia's face as she wept. Her brother, her best friend, the man she loved more than anyone in the world, was dead. He had always protected her. Anyone that messed with her in school had to deal with her big brother. Even in elementary school, he could take on any bully. It didn't matter if they were older or bigger, they feared the wrath of her brother.

She gasped for air through sobs as the tears continued to flow.

"Mia...Mia..."

Through overwhelming grief, she heard someone calling her name and felt her face being wiped, but she no longer was capable of uttering a sound. All Mia wanted was her brother. She felt a prick in her arm, and then darkness descended around her.

Chapter 10

Hearing noises outside, Mia attempted to open her swollen eyes, but they only opened a slit. She ran her fingertips over them and separated her stuck-together eyelashes. The horror of the prior night flashed into her mind, and her sense of loss was beyond tears.

She swung her feet over the bed's edge, stood, and trudged barefooted to the bathroom down the hall. Locking the door, she went to the sink and washed her face. Mia looked in the mirror and saw the image of a pale-faced woman with heavy, swollen eyes and matted-down, brown hair. As she continued staring at the unrecognizable image, she noticed all she had on was her underwear. It didn't matter to her who had undressed her. Mia felt numb, and nothing seemed important anymore. She touched her injured side. No serious pain.

Mia left the bathroom and ambled back to her bed. She crawled under the covers, closed her eyes, and fell back to sleep.

When she awoke again, it was dark outside. The

nightstand lamp was on. She heard a creaking and looked in that direction.

Vince rose from a chair and came to her. He brushed hair away from her pale face. "How are you doing?"

Mia just gazed at him without answering his question.

"Do you feel hungry?"

She shook her head.

"Let's see if you can drink something." He put an arm under her neck and raised her into a sitting position. With his other hand, he took a glass of water from the nightstand and held it against her lips.

Mia slowly took a few sips.

"Can you drink a little more?"

She shook her head.

Vince put the glass back on the nightstand and laid her head on the pillow. He brought a chair over to the bed and sat down. "Mia, I am so sorry for your loss. Is there anything I can do for you?"

She wordlessly glared at him.

He stroked her cheek. "We haven't picked up any sounds that would indicate your enemy is close by. Do you know anything about the hole in the back yard?"

Remembering her Aunt Thelma, her mother, and an unfamiliar man had buried something there, Mia nodded yes.

"I've heard that some of the stuff your father stole before he went to prison was never recovered. Was it buried there?"

"No," she mumbled.

"What I'm getting at is...do we need to be concerned about who dug that hole?"

Mia shrugged.

"Maybe you're not up to answering any questions. Would you like me to go away?"

"Yes."

Vince stood, kissed her on the forehead, and left the bedroom.

* * *

The next time Mia opened her eyes, only light streaming under the door illuminated her room. She stared at the ceiling. Grief pierced through her as she thought about Andy, but she needed to pull herself together. Had she been the one killed, Andy would have stopped at nothing to find the murderer. He deserved no less. Mia resolved she would risk everything to hunt down the killer and give him the same fate he had unmercifully handed her brother. But first she needed to figure out "why." *What have Andy and I done that would warrant that? Andy's killer is either someone we've worked for or someone we're working for.* Andy always dealt with those people, not Mia. *Maybe I know one of them without realizing it.*

Her stomach growled. There wasn't any food at the farm, but Vince had offered her some. One of his men must have gone shopping. On that thought, she climbed out of bed and looked around for something to put on. Her jogging suit was nowhere in sight and neither was her duffle bag. She checked the closet and saw her duffle bag and purse on the shelf. Her skirt, blouse, jeans, t-shirt, and jogging suit had been hung up. On the floor stood her heels and athletic shoes.

She slipped on her jogging suit and athletic shoes and headed downstairs, holding onto the railing for balance. The back porch light shined through a window, helping her navigate her way to the kitchen. Mia turned on the light over the sink and saw a loaf of bread, bags of chips, and fruit on the counter. Opening the fridge door, she was surprised by all the food. Every shelf was full along with the meat and vegetable drawers.

Mia proceeded to make a sandwich. Grabbing it, a bottle of water, and a bag of chips, she sat down at the table and began to eat. She had just taken her second bite when she heard feet pounding down the stairs.

"You must be feeling better." Vince looked like he'd slept in his sweats and t-shirt.

She finished crunching on a chip. "A little."

"I'm still concerned about the hole in the backyard. Are you up to telling me what you know about it?"

Mia swallowed the food in her mouth. "Yes. Let me finish the sandwich first."

Vince wandered through the first floor, looking out windows, as Mia ate.

When she was through, the early morning sunlight flowed into the kitchen. "Did you sleep at all last night?"

"Yes. I slept in your bedroom."

"My bedroom?"

"The pink walls, ruffles on the curtains, and stuffed animals kind of gave it away. You must be sleeping in the bedroom either used by your aunt or your mother."

"My mother. Are your guys sleeping in the house?"

"Walt is. Owen is in the van, keeping watch."

"You intend to help me find Andy's killer?"

"Yes. That person is also Ethan's killer. We're on the same side now."

"Vince, Andy didn't deliver all the uncut diamonds, but we were going to fix that. Except for maybe the guy he shorted, I have no idea who would want to kill us. Andy set up our jobs. I never saw the men, and they didn't know I existed. Yeah, they knew Andy had someone working with him, but not that it was his sister. People don't even know Andy has a sister. My father didn't even show me as a next of kin when he went to prison. He never told anyone about me. But this last week, Andy thought someone was on to me. He didn't want me to be alone at night outside. He even wanted me to make sure you walked me to the lobby of my building the night I went to your house."

"I take it the guy who grabbed you wasn't just a random attacker."

"Probably not. During the week, I received several calls from an 'unidentified caller.' Once, he left me a message something like—'Mia, Mia, why you?' Any idea what he meant by that?"

"My guess would be that the man discovered who you really were and didn't like it."

"Maybe it was to scare me…or to rile up Andy. Andy's always protected me."

"Mia, I'd be happy to take over that job."

"We started out using each other. You were looking for your cousin's killer, and I was looking for the safe in your house. Yes, we have a common goal now, but let's not pretend it's more than that. Let's just be ourselves. Okay?"

"The night you were in my bedroom, I wasn't

playing a role. I wanted nothing more than you. I've gone over that night several times in my mind, and I can't think of anything I did that suddenly caused you to end everything. Can you enlighten me?"

"You did everything perfectly. Nothing wrong. But you were my mark. I don't get emotionally involved with marks. When a job is done, so is whatever relationship I developed to obtain information."

"So what am I now?"

A faint smile creased Mia's lips. "Not a mark. You're an associate, someone I hope I can trust. But Vince, are you trying to tell me you didn't invite me to your home for any other reason than to have my company? Come on. You planted a bug on my purse, and you lied about who you were."

"I wanted to go out with you regardless. Having a dual purpose made it difficult. I'll take trusted associate for now."

"Good. Let me tell you about the hole. When I was around ten, Aunt Thelma, my mom, and a guy I had never seen before, dug that hole and buried a wooden box about the size of a foot locker in it. Right before the guy arrived, Mom ushered Andy and me upstairs and told us to stay there until she came to get us. Mom had never done that before. As kids, we wanted to know what was going on. Looking out Mom's window, we saw a big, white truck pull down the lane and drive to the back of the house. Andy and I hurried to his bedroom and watched the whole thing from there.

"After the guy left, Mom came upstairs, and we asked her about it. She said a friend wanted something stored at Aunt Thelma's. Thelma didn't want it standing around, so they buried it. Andy thought they had buried a treasure and wanted to dig it up the next day," Mia said with a soft laugh. "At the time, I thought it was weird that they buried it in middle of the dirt driveway when there's a pasture and plenty of ground among the trees. Years later, I understood. Every once and a while when I saw a dip in that section of the driveway, either Mom or Aunt Thelma would fill it with dirt until everything became even and the ground became hard. No one could see anything had ever been buried there. Great way to hide something you don't want found. Whoever unburied it needed to have known the exact location."

"How often do you come here?"

"I haven't been here since Aunt Thelma died, six years ago."

"And Andy?"

"He comes here sometimes to unwind and solve problems."

"The hole looks fresh. Could Andy have dug up the box?"

"Possibly. If he did, he never mentioned it to me, and I think he would've filled the hole. Maybe the guy who brought it here dug it up."

"Did your aunt and mom ever talk about it?"

"After one or the other put more dirt in the hole, they whispered a lot. To tell you the truth, I had completely forgotten about it. Otherwise, I would've dodged that pile of dirt instead of leaping over it right into the hole." Mia fisted her hand and tapped her head. "Dumb. Dumb. You never would've been able to find me if I got inside that barn."

"I doubt that. You'd have to surface sometime for water and food."

"Good point."

An overwhelming grief suddenly surged through Mia's body and tears filled her eyes again.

Vince clutched her hand. "Mia, what's wrong?"

"I'd like you to do something for me." Her voice sounded heavy with despair.

"What? Anything."

Her lips quavered. A few tears flowed down her cheeks. "I'd like you to make arrangements...for my...brother's body." She sniffled, picked up a napkin, and wiped her face. "I want him to be buried by my mother and aunt in a cemetery about five miles from here....I can't...I can't remember the name of the cemetery."

Vince stood and enveloped her in his arms. "Don't worry. I'll take care of it. But it might be a few days, if not longer, before his body can be released. I'll handle everything."

"Thank you."

Vince led her back upstairs and tucked her under the covers. He caressed her damp cheek before leaving the room.

Chapter 11

Mia slept for a while and then got up and showered. Berating herself for sleeping when she should be hunting for Andy's killer, she put on her jeans and a t-shirt. She resolved to keep her tears at bay.

Heading down the stairs, she heard Vince and Owen talking in the kitchen. When she walked in, both men turned toward her.

"Would you like some lunch?" Vince asked. "Walt made a pasta salad, or I could make you a sandwich."

"Pasta salad sounds good." Mia got a soda out of the fridge, grabbed a bowl and utensils, sat at the table, and helped herself.

"Vince, I'll get to work on what we discussed." Owen went out the back door.

"How's your side?"

"A little painful when I touch it, but not bad." Mia scooped up a forkful of salad. "What was Owen talking about?"

"He's going to fill in the hole before someone else falls into it. Then we should leave. You'll be safer at my place, and since we haven't heard or seen anything suspicious after you arrived here, there's a strong possibility the culprit doesn't know you own this place or you were raised here. But whoever dug up that hole knows about this place. The farm has too many places for thugs to hide. Do you agree?"

"Remember...the text I received on Friday—the one I thought Andy sent—said 'Run, Mia, Run. Meet you at our place.' Whoever sent that had to know about this place."

"Not necessarily. He might've planned to follow you, but with your clever escape, you probably lost him." Vince rubbed his chin. "Text? Is it on your cell phone upstairs?"

"Yes. It's a burner phone without GPS. Andy and I often use them for jobs." She smiled at him. "You know...like robbing you. When I left the fundraiser, I threw away my smart phone because of GPS. Wait...I assumed that text came from Andy's burner. I never checked."

"You only used that phone to contact Andy's?"

"Yes."

"Is it okay if I get it and have Walt look it over?"

Mia nodded as she continued eating.

Vince left. A few seconds later, the front door opened and closed. When he returned to the kitchen, he said, "A 'no caller ID' sent the text. Walt might be able to locate the number associated with the caller."

"How did that person get a hold of my burner number?"

Vince shrugged. "I still want to take you to my place."

"We're not going to be able to find the assassin if I hide from him. It might work better if I go back to my apartment. But first, I need to replace my cell phone. I'll have my number installed in it. The killer might be the 'unidentified caller.' What do you think?"

"Possibly. According to Kirby, it's either the old boss or the new one. My initial plan is to claim the uncut diamonds have been stolen from my home. Whoever arranged for Andy and his associate to pull the job, will want the diamonds. He might believe Andy swiped them before the..." Vince hesitated.

Mia finished his sentence. "...Explosion."

"And Mia, you need to look more like yourself before you return to your place."

Mia knew she looked a mess. "What would you suggest?"

"Come to my place. Stay there while I report the robbery. Police will show up. Then when you're up to it, go to your apartment. But I must insist on going with you. I need to know you're safe."

"Won't the police question everyone at your house?"

"Yes. The servants will believe a robbery took place. To make the robbery appear as real as possible, how would you have stolen the diamonds?"

"In the heists Andy and I did, he always took the stolen goods. Had the plan to steal uncut diamonds from your house played out, I never would've seen them." She tapped her fingertips together. "Had Andy snatched them before the explosion, he could've made things right with the old boss and made some arrangements with the new boss. There would be no reason for either of them to want him dead. The new and old boss need to believe I stole them after the explosion. Since Andy is the person they hired to crack the safe, those bosses might not know his associate possesses that skill. So even if they heard LeMonte's uncut diamonds had been taken, there's a chance they wouldn't believe I was the thief. If they come after me, I might need them to think I have the diamonds...for leverage. The best way to convince them would be to explain how I accomplished the theft. In order to sound realistic, I'll go with you to your house and steal the diamonds."

"And how are you planning to do that?"

"Okay, we're going to have to do a little role playing. I'll be your house guest. Let your servants and guards know that. Like last time, we'll have dinner on your balcony, but you'll have to make sure your cook doesn't see my face. Puffy eyes don't work for a romantic dinner. Oh...do you have someone constantly monitoring your surveillance cameras?"

"Only when there are guests in the house."

"I lack Andy's ability to take care of that type of security. He'd always told me what switch to pull, wire to undo, or guard to keep busy. I guess that's going to have to be your job. How can I disable your surveillance cameras?"

"I'll do that for you."

"Can you be cool about it so no one suspects?"

A crooked smile creased his lips. "I can handle it."

"Good. Then I won't worry about that. This is how it's going to go down." She became very focused. "After dinner, we'll have drinks in your front parlor and wait for the servants to retreat to their private rooms. They're on the other side of the kitchen, right?"

"Yes."

"Then we'll get ready for bed, but you won't turn

on your laser security system. The bed in the guest room you assigned me won't be slept in. I'll sleep with you."

"This robbery thing is starting to sound pretty good."

"Once you are sound asleep, I'll creep out of bed and go down and rob your safe. The next morning, I'll go to work. Then sometime during the day, you'll discover your safe has been robbed and report it. The maid will know I slept with you, and you'll claim I was with you all night. The police will probably want to ask me a few questions, but I have a clean record, and I certainly wouldn't have left any fingerprints. How does that sound?"

"One question. Where will the diamonds be after you've stolen them?"

"In my safe deposit box. Completely out of your reach."

"Mia?"

"Okay. They'll be in your house someplace. You'll have to find a spot for them. Once the police have checked everything out, you might want to put them back in the safe. Oh, I'm going to need a stethoscope, latex gloves, and some clothes. I can't show up to work wearing the same outfit I wore on Friday."

"Do you think you'll feel up to going to work tomorrow?"

"Probably not, but my eyes should look normal by then, and if I seem a little sluggish, people will just think I had wild weekend. Vince, since Kirby said the culprit knows me, I want to carry on a normal routine. Who knows? It could be one of Feinstein's clients. I doubt anyone will shoot me at work, and I won't leave the building during lunch. My car is still parked at the Marriott. Could you have one of your men take it to your house? But make sure it isn't rigged to explode. I don't want anyone else…"

"I'll have your car delivered. There's a department store not far from here. I'll go there and buy you a dress and a shear nightgown."

Mia shook her head. "Vince, remember we're just associates." Even though she was attracted to him, she felt she couldn't handle more than a business relationship while searching for Andy's killer.

Vince studied her for a minute and then said, "To make this heist look legit, I don't intend to send anyone to buy a stethoscope. I'll do it and also pick up latex gloves."

"There's got to be several medical supply places someplace in New Haven. If you can find the one that's closest, I could go in and buy that stuff."

"You don't want me to do that?"

"No. In case the heist ends up in the newspaper, your picture could be alongside the article. Doubt anyone would put that together, but it's better not to take a chance. And, like you said, I don't look like myself."

Vince tapped on his cell phone. "There's one two blocks from the department store. I'll take you. How soon do you want to go?"

Mia glanced at her watch. "It's three-fifteen. If we want to pull this off tonight, we need to get going. Let me just grab a wig and a cap."

Within an hour, Vince and Mia had purchased everything and were back at the farm.

Before leaving for Vince's place, Mia fixed her hair and dressed in the same outfit she wore to the fundraiser. Then she gathered up her belongings, put them in the duffle bag, and headed downstairs.

Wondering when she'd see the farm again, she gazed into the kitchen and the image of Andy sitting at the table flashed into her head. A tidal wave of grief struck her again. She swallowed hard, turned, and forced herself to walk out the front door without shedding any more tears.

Chapter 12

Once they reached New York City, Vince stopped at a T-Mobile store. Mia went inside, purchased another phone, and had the sales rep transfer her old number to it.

Shortly before eight, they arrived at Vince's house. He carried her duffle bag along with the purchases and showed her to one of the guest rooms. "Will this do?"

"Very nicely." She set her purse on the bureau.

"I don't mean to rush you, but dinner will be ready in ten minutes. Chicken Cordon Bleu. I requested main course only. Then you won't need to hide your face as often."

"Sounds good. You set that up while I was purchasing another phone?"

Vince shrugged. "Since you want to go to work in the morning, I didn't want this to be a late night."

"Give me a few minutes to freshen up."

"I'll do the same."

Fifteen minutes later, Vince escorted her through

the house to the balcony. Like before, the table was elegantly set. "In order not to have your face seen, I suggest that you admire the garden while my chef delivers the food. I'll tap my fork on my plate when I see him coming."

"Got it. How about the security cameras?"

"They started malfunctioning shortly after we arrived." A faint smile crossed his lips. "They might be out of commission for four or five hours."

"What a shame," Mia said with a solemn expression.

Vince's eyes moved to something behind her, and then he tapped his plate.

"I love your garden." Mia rose and went to the railing and gazed out at the magnificent backyard while she heard soft clanging sounds behind her.

Vince appeared by her side and handed her a glass of white wine. He clicked her glass. "To our new relationship."

"Our *business* relationship."

When Mia ate the last morsel, she looked at Vince's half-full plate. "Wow. I should've slowed down. It's not ladylike to devour everything before your date has finished."

"Who says that?"

"You might find this hard to believe, but my mother and Aunt Thelma constantly drilled proper manners into me."

"I don't find it hard to believe at all. There is nothing about you that would indicate you are anything but a lady. What I have found hard to believe is that the charming Mia Sloan has a second job—one that requires sneaking around at night." He ate another bite and then downed the wine in his glass. "Did you use the word 'date' to describe me?" He filled their wine glasses.

"Metaphorically speaking. Nothing more."

As the maid came to clear off the table, Vince stood, took Mia's arm, and led her into the front parlor. Several bottles stood on a side table along with goblets and an assortment of liqueur glasses.

Mia sat down on the couch and gazed at the low flames in the fireplace. "Do you always use your fireplace?"

"No, but it brings ambiance to the room, and since we might be here for a while, I thought you'd enjoy it." He went to the side table. "Would you prefer Chartreuse, Sherry, or Brandy?"

"Sherry, please."

Vince filled a sherry glass for Mia, poured a Brandy for himself, and sat down next to her. They gazed at the fire and slowly sipped their drinks. Vince occasionally rose to stoke the fire.

"How will you know when the servants retire?"

"I'll check the kitchen in half an hour."

As they waited, Mia thought about cracking the safe. That was a job Andy normally handled, but there were occasions when a constantly monitored surveillance system required him to spend his time keeping it disabled. Then Mia took over the task of breaking into the safe. She was skilled, but not at Andy's level. He never needed a stethoscope, but she seldom could do it without one. To get her mind off of her impending job, she asked, "Was Walt able to find out the number behind 'No Caller ID'?"

"Yes, but he hasn't been able to determine who the number belongs to. He's going to work on it this evening. It might be a burner phone."

"Maybe it's a Feinstein client. Can you give me the number?"

"I had already planned to do that."

"Since I normally take a cab to work, I intend to take one tomorrow."

"Then I'll have your car taken to your apartment's parking garage."

She gave him a puzzled look. "But you can't get into the garage."

"That won't be a problem. It'll be parked on level two. A tail will be close by your cab but a distance away where it won't be easily spotted. After work, I'll be waiting for you in the lobby of your apartment building."

"Do you really think it's necessary for you to stay at my apartment?"

"Absolutely." Vince rose and left the room.

Figuring he was going to check on the status of his employees in the kitchen, Mia stood and wandered into the dining room and looked at the painting with the heavy frame. She assumed the safe was behind it, but she wasn't absolutely sure. Still, she knew it was in that room, and she'd have time to search for it if it wasn't behind that painting. She realized Vince could tell her where it was, but she wanted it to seem like a real heist, and he had already partially spoiled that by disabling the surveillance cameras. Mia would've liked to have done that herself. Even though she no longer wanted to be a thief, she still liked the rush it gave her. Escaping from difficult situations elicited fear and thrills.

"Admiring the paintings?" Vince interrupted her thoughts.

"Yes." She turned toward him and whispered, "I

was trying to figure out how much they might be worth."

"Miss Sloan..." He leaned closer to her ear. "Are you already contemplating your next heist?"

She gave him a mischievous smile. "Possibly." Mia moved to the next painting. "How are they doing in the kitchen?"

"All cleaned up and the lights are turned off. So what do you say we go to bed?"

"What did you buy me to sleep in?"

"You'll have to wait and see. I've moved your things into my bedroom."

"You are very efficient, Mr. Tolbert."

Vince's brow rose as he gazed at her. "I do like to please."

As they headed to the stairwell, he turned off the lights but then reconsidered and flipped some back on.

"Do you always leave lights on when you go to bed?"

"No, but I want you to be able to see to do your job."

"Turn off all the lights like your normal routine. I have a flashlight in my purse which I intend to use." Mia watched him go back and flip off the remaining lights.

In his bedroom, he handed her one of the bags. "You can use the bathroom first, unless of course, you don't mind sharing."

"Business associates. Remember?" Mia carried the bag into the bathroom and locked the door. She pulled the nightgown out of the bag. To her surprise, it was modest—a three-quarter sleeved, high-necked, mid-calf length, soft blue nightgown. Staring at it, she thought it was perfect for the job. She felt something else in the bag and lifted out a pair of slippers. Mia looked at the size on the nightgown and slippers. *How does Vince know my sizes?*

She changed into the new purchases and washed up for bed. Since she lacked a toothbrush, she pushed some of his toothpaste on her index finger and rubbed it on her teeth.

Mia stepped out of the bathroom. "Your turn."

He eyed her up and down as they passed each other.

After he closed the bathroom door, Mia checked her watch—10:36 p.m.—and decided she'd head to the safe at 11:00. She looked at the bed and saw a cell phone and alarm clock on the nightstand on the left side. Assuming that was the side Vince slept on, she stretched out on the other side of the bed. She had sometimes shared beds with marks when she knew they were too intoxicated to be amorous. Most were asleep when she climbed under the covers. Mia shook her head, recalling the next morning they believed they had a great time in bed. *I've never slept with a guy who wasn't a mark or a boyfriend before.*

"I don't often walk out of my bathroom to find a gorgeous woman in my bed."

Mia turned and leaned on her side. "Okay, you don't *often* find a woman in your bed." She slightly moved up and down on it. "That means sometimes you do. So this mattress must be well broken in."

"No. Not at all. I can't recall the last time I had company in this bedroom." His eyes bore into her swollen ones.

It didn't go unnoticed by Mia that he said, "this bedroom." She wondered if he went to a guest bedroom if he had someone in the house for overnight romance. She rolled back on her back, trying to snap those thoughts out of her mind. Vince was her business associate. Nothing more.

Mia glanced at her watch. "Show time." She got up and looked for the plastic bag with the name of the medical supply store on it. Seeing it on the chair in the corner, she put the stethoscope around her neck and tucked it under the nightgown. Then she pulled out a pair of gloves and pushed them into her bra which she had left on for that very purpose. Next, she retrieved her flashlight from her purse and headed toward the door.

"Do you want me to tell you where the safe is?"

"No. I'm quite capable of finding it on my own."

"Okay, but don't forget I offered."

Even though the servants were in their quarters, Mia still crept downstairs with only the moonlight shining through the windows, illuminating her way. She wanted to go through the same moves she would've used had it been a real heist.

When she reached the dining room archway, she slipped on the gloves, turned on her mini-LED flashlight, and went to the painting with the heavy frame. Assuming it was hinged, Mia gripped the corner of it, raised it, and discovered she had been wrong. The painting was hung by a wire and concealed nothing. *Okay, bad guess.* She checked behind every painting. No safe. *How is that possible?* She gazed around the room and didn't see another spot where a safe could be hidden. It was the only room in the house with a laser security system. Then Vince's amused face bounced into her head when he asked if she wanted the location of the safe.

Mia certainly didn't intend to run up the stairs and ask him. After all, she was a thief and should at least know how to find a safe. *What would Andy do?* She went to the front parlor and looked behind all the paintings. No safe. Then she moved to the den and began the same process. *Bingo.* A small safe was behind a picture near the desk.

Thinking the sophisticated security system in the dining room was just a ruse, she proceeded to crack the safe. Mia had it opened in less than a minute. Pleased with herself, she saw a stack of documents and figured the diamonds were tucked somewhere on the far side. She pulled out some papers. Not seeing a bag that would contain uncut diamonds—in fact, not seeing anything but papers—she removed everything. No diamonds. Not wanting to leave any sign that she had opened that safe, she carefully replaced all documents in the same order they had previously been in, locked the safe, and re-hung the picture, making sure it was level.

Mia had been on heists with Andy and a few with her father before he went to jail where there were several safes in a home or building, each one for a specific purpose. She moved to the back parlor and eyed the space. With two sets of balcony doors and six windows in the room, she couldn't imagine a safe that held a fortune in diamonds could be there. Yet, she went around and checked under everything that hung on the walls.

Feeling frustrated, she headed back into the dining room. *It has to be in here someplace. That's the only logical explanation.* Mia wished she had Andy's exceptional skill in locating hard-to-find safes. She wandered around the room, shining the flashlight over the oak flooring, studying each plank for anything unusual like a small spot where a tool or knife could be inserted to raise it. A few times, she bent down and felt the floor. The table and chairs sat on a Persian rug. Since it would be a daunting task to open a safe hidden under there, Mia decided to look behind the furniture against the walls. Shining her flashlight behind each piece, she didn't see anything unusual.

Concerned she might have to ask for Vince's help, she rubbed her head, trying to recall all the strange places where Andy had found safes. Then she noticed the dining room fireplace was a gas one, not a regular one like in the parlor. Her eyes moved to the three-section mirror above the fireplace, embellished with elegant gold-leaf scrolling separating the sections. The mirror extended the width of the ornate mantel at least two feet beyond the firebox on each side.

Mia went to the mirror and carefully examined the scrolls. She couldn't see any lines that indicated a section could be raised. Still, she shined her flashlight around the edge of the mirror and saw a small space less than half an inch behind it. She wrapped her fingers around the edge and attempted to raise it. It wouldn't budge. Then she did the same thing to the other side of the mirror with the same results. Wondering if there could be another way to get behind part of it, she ran her fingers around the edge and, at the bottom of the right section, she felt a spot where she could insert her fingers. With them in that hole, she attempted to slide that section of the mirror away from the scroll. She beamed when it moved, but it wouldn't go any farther than a few inches. Thinking it could be hinged, she tried to raise it. It moved easily. *Voilà!*

The safe was recessed in the wall. Now she faced another problem, she could reach the dial, but she was too short to crack it. Mia took a chair from the table, stood on it, and went to work. Within three minutes, she had the black velvet bag containing the uncut diamonds in her hand. After putting the chair back, she glanced around the room to make sure everything looked as pristine as when she had entered.

Mia headed up the stairs with a big smile on her face. Before she opened the door to Vince's room, she hid her hand that held the bag in the folds of her nightgown and tried to look discouraged.

As she entered the room, Vince, who was stretched out on the bed with his hands behind his head, looked at her. "I said I'd tell you were it was. Give up?"

She dropped the velvet bag on the bed.

A puzzled look crossed his face. "You found the safe?"

"Did you expect me to fail?"

"To tell you the truth...yes. What took you so long?"

"I thought I'd give you a little while to fall asleep before I came back in here, so I sat in front of the parlor fireplace, enjoying the smoldering ashes."

"So it wasn't because you searched behind paintings in all the rooms?"

Mia tilted her head. "You told me you had disabled the surveillance cameras."

"I have, but you're not the first thief that has found some way to enter the house. However, you are the first one who wouldn't have left empty-handed."

"Well, I am exceptionally skilled," she said with a

straight face, thinking she only found it because she wasn't in a time crunch, like she suspected others had been. "But you'll have to give up that clever safe location when you report the stolen diamonds."

"If the robbery leads us to Ethan's killer, it'll be worth that cost." Vince rose, picked up the bag of diamonds, and slipped them into a bureau drawer.

Mia put the flashlight, stethoscope, and latex gloves in her purse. Then she headed to the bathroom to wash up before going to bed. When she climbed under the covers, Mia saw Vince's eyes were closed but soon discovered he wasn't asleep.

He pulled her into his arms.

"Vince, this isn't the way business associates behave."

"Yeah, I know." He held her tightly.

She liked being in his arms, but Mia wanted to stay focused on the job they had to do. "You're hurting my side," she lied.

Vince released her. "Oh, sorry. I forgot."

Mia rolled over on her other side and fell asleep.

Chapter 13

As if she had set an alarm clock, Mia opened her eyes at 7:00, the exact time she had planned to get up, and found herself snuggled next to Vince. She carefully untangled herself from his arms and eased out of bed. Mia grabbed her purse and the remaining plastic bag and headed into the bathroom.

Trying to be quiet, she quickly showered. With her hair wrapped in a towel, she looked at her face in the mirror. It still appeared slightly pale, but her eyes were no longer swollen. Using the same method she did the prior day, she brushed her teeth, and then, doubting Vince would have a hair dryer, she vigorously rubbed her hair in the towel, hoping to dry it a little. She ran a comb through her damp tresses and then rummaged through her purse for a large barrette, an item she had often used to keep her hair out of her eyes when working with Andy. Mia pulled back part of her locks and clipped on the barrette. Thinking she didn't look too bad, she applied her makeup. She pulled the dress Vince had purchased out of the bag and slipped it on. Gazing in the mirror, she thought he had pretty good taste. It was a well-tailored, light teal dress made of a soft fabric that didn't show any wrinkles.

She padded out of the bathroom in her bare feet and saw an empty bed. Wondering where Vince had gone, Mia sat down and slipped on her heels. She put the strap of her duffle over her shoulder, picked up her purse, and looked around the room. Even though she didn't have very many things with her, she wanted to make sure she had collected all of them. Out of curiosity, she looked in the drawer where Vince had stuck the uncut diamonds. They weren't there. To keep them safe, Mia figured he had put them into the safe in the den—a safe he didn't know she had also discovered.

Going down the stairs, Mia saw Vince, dressed in sweats, stepping out of the dining room and wondered if he had checked the safe to make sure she hadn't snatched anything else.

"Wow. Do you look great," Vince said, walking toward her.

"Thanks for the dress."

"My pleasure. We'll be having breakfast in the dining room." He took her duffle bag and put it near the front door.

As they went through the archway, Mia saw the table had been set for two, and a basket of various types of rolls and butter was on it. Vince pulled out a chair for her—the same one she had stood on earlier.

Once Mia was seated, he asked, "Coffee?"

"Yes, please."

Vince lifted up the coffee carafe on the sideboard. As he poured, a maid came in carrying two plates and placed them on the table.

"Will there be anything else, sir?"

Vince eyed the food. "No, Martha, you haven't missed a thing. Thank you."

The maid slightly nodded and left the room.

Mia stared at the fried eggs, ham, and hash browns on her plate. "Do you always eat this much for breakfast?"

"Not always." He smiled. "Sometimes I have a side of pancakes to go with it."

Since she had so quickly devoured her food last night, Mia paced herself, not wanting to finish the meal before Vince. "When I didn't return to my table at the fundraiser, what was the reaction?"

"Lorraine was worried you might have eaten something that didn't agree with you and checked the women's restroom, and then she went to the parking garage to see if your car was gone. Lewis told her he noticed you looking at your phone and thought maybe your aunt wasn't doing well. They were both confused that your car was still in the parking garage. Lewis tried to call you and ended up leaving a message."

"And what were you doing all that time?"

"Checking text messages for updates on your location. I took Lorraine home."

"She must've loved that."

"Well…she didn't seem disappointed that you had abandoned her." Vince finished off his meal and then pulled a ring out of his pocket. "I want you to wear this."

Mia looked at the ring. It was the same one she had given back to him. "Why? Lewis knows Oliver LeMonte had let me borrow it, and I returned it. He's going to think something is up if he sees it on my finger after I told him I couldn't afford it."

"That's the point. If the killer should be someone associated with Feinstein & Dawson—maybe a client—seeing a ring on your finger that Mia Sloan, an employee, couldn't afford and then hearing about a robbery at LeMonte's house, it could easily make that person believe you were the thief. The culprit already knows you engage in that type of activity."

She reached across the table, took the ring from him, and placed it on her finger. "Do you think it could be Lewis?"

"I doubt that, but I never suspected the lovely Miss Sloan whom I saw at Feinstein's party could have a shady side to her. I'm normally a good judge of character. I must be slipping. At work, suspect everyone. No exceptions. On second thought, take Lorraine off the list. That's a gal who doesn't know how to keep secrets."

Mia already knew that and wondered what Lorraine had blabbed to Vince to give him that impression.

Vince stuck his hand in his pocket and pulled out a folded piece of paper and gave it to her. "That's the number associated with "No Caller ID."

"I'll check it out as soon as I get to work. Oh, I just remembered. I told Lewis I'd go to lunch with him today. I keep putting him off. I'd rather not do it again."

"Lorraine mentioned you had a lunch date with him. She thinks you two are an item."

Mia rolled her eyes and shook her head.

"Don't drive anywhere with him. Go to that Italian restaurant that's right across the street from your office building."

Mia disliked being given orders, but an unknown killer was after her. She needed Vince and his manpower to keep her safe.

* * *

Mia entered Feinstein's lobby. "Hey, Lorraine, sorry I left you at the fundraiser. I suddenly felt sick and went to the restroom. After losing my dinner, I felt even worse and took a taxi to my aunt's house. With all the medicines she takes, I knew there'd be something there that would help. Did you have any trouble finding a ride home?"

"No. Things worked out perfectly. Vince Tolbert took me home. He is so dreamy. I gave him my phone number. Hope he'll call. If I don't hear from him in a few days, I'm going to call him. One of my neighbors is having a party. That'll give me a great excuse to ask him out. Don't you think?"

"Absolutely. I better get to work."

Before she got settled at her desk, Lewis strolled in. "What happened to you at the fundraiser?"

After repeating the same explanation she had given to Lorraine, she said, "But now I'm feeling one-hundred percent."

"Good. Are we still on for lunch today?"

"Yes. How would it be if we went to the Italian restaurant across the street? I haven't eaten there for a while, and I especially like their eggplant parmesan." Mia moved a stack of files to the top of her desk.

"How about going at one?" Lewis's eyes lowered to her hand.

"That works for me."

"I thought you gave back the ring."

"I did, but when my aunt noticed I wasn't wearing it, she asked me about it. After I filled her in, she insisted on giving me a sizeable down payment. I had no idea she had that kind of money. Just goes to show you, never judge—what's that saying? Oh—a book by its cover."

"You should have told me you were going to purchase it. I could've arranged a discount for you."

"I lost my cell phone so I couldn't call you, but I did manage to get a ten percent discount."

"I could've done a little better than that. Did you find your phone?"

"No. I got a new one. Same number, but all my contacts are gone."

"I'll give you my number at lunch. See you then."

Mia leaned back in her chair, thinking about recent clients she had dealt with. None seemed like thieves or killers, but appearances could be deceptive. Andy had told her most of the guys that had hired him wore Armani suits. Mia assumed that meant they had a well-off circle of friends. They'd need a cover to pretend how they made their fortune. Something respectable. Dealing in stolen goods wouldn't work.

She pulled out the number Vince had given her and checked her data base. No match.

Mia felt tears well in her eyes as she wondered why Andy had been killed before the heist. *Could his death have been unrelated to the diamond capers?* She couldn't imagine it. Since she was also in danger, the motive had to be something she had done with Andy.

A memory sparked Mia's concern. Andy had mentioned he had a "last resort" method to obtain the money he needed to get out of the jam if they couldn't get the diamonds. *What did that mean? Had Andy dug up that box and found something interesting in it— something that the guy who buried it never wanted to surface? Maybe some kind of evidence that could land him in jail? Would Aunt Thelma and Mom help him bury something like that?*

Questions kept swirling around in Mia's head, but she doubted she'd be able to find any answers until someone made a move on her. Mia thumbed through the top folder on her desk to get her head into her job. It didn't work. Her thoughts drifted back to Andy's death. *Why?*

At exactly one o'clock, Lewis tapped on her door and opened it. "Ready?"

Mia grabbed her purse and headed to the restaurant on the other side of the street.

While they ate, they talked about a couple of projects they were working on together and Lewis's upcoming trip to Italy to visit a friend, but Mia sensed something was off. When Lewis spoke he seldom looked at her face. His eyes kept glancing around as if he was looking for someone. He had been asking her out for years. She had gone with him to lunch before but always in a group. This was the first time she had gone with him alone. He scanned the restaurant again and seemed a little jittery and nervous.

Why is he acting like that? "Lewis, is something wrong?"

He cleared his throat. "No…No. I'm just running behind on a project."

"You should have told me. We could've gone to lunch another day. Can I help you on the project?"

"I have a few people working on it now, but I probably should get back."

After paying the bill, they walked back to the agency. Mia kept trying to stir up a conversation on the way but only managed to get a few words out of Lewis.

Back in her office, an unnerving thought sprang into her mind. *Could Lewis be the culprit? Had he expected a thug to show up—someone who would've escorted me out the back door? Someone given the job to make sure I joined my brother?* Even if that had been his intent, the place was too crowded to pull it off. Mia couldn't envision Lewis having a dark side. She couldn't imagine him packing or even knowing how to shoot a gun.

On her taxi ride home, Mia kept an eye out for a tail. No cars stood out. Yet, she sensed she was being watched. Probably Vince's men.

She climbed out of the taxi and grabbed her duffle bag.

As she stepped into the lobby, Vince walked toward her. "How was your work day?"

"Unusual."

His brow furrowed, and then he gestured toward a man, dressed in white and holding a metal box. "I brought dinner." Vince whispered, "It's safer to eat in your apartment."

After they entered her apartment, the man in white set the table and put foil-wrapped containers in her oven to keep them warm and other containers in the fridge. Then he left with the metal box.

Vince lifted two bottles of wine out of his sack. "Where's your corkscrew?"

"Second drawer."

He opened a bottle and filled two wine glasses.

When they were seated on the couch, Vince toasted. "To finding the killer."

Mia took a sip. "I had expected to get a call from the police after you reported the theft...asking me if I saw anything suspicious—stuff like that—but nothing. What time did you report it?"

"I didn't. Since there would be no reason for me to even check the safe, I thought it would be better for Oliver to report it. He'll be in town sometime tonight. He's coming to cut some of the diamonds. We'll know when he discovers the diamonds are missing."

Mia briefly wondered if Oliver would look in the den safe before reporting them missing, but then she figured he wouldn't. *After all, why would any family member move the diamonds from one safe to another when the dining room has the top-notch, sophisticated, security system?*

"What was unusual at work today?"

"Lewis. I went to lunch with him, but something was definitely troubling him. He kept looking around. Hardly paid any attention to me, which was very unusual. Outside of that, I checked the number you gave me and went through my list of clients. I came up with zilch. How did your day go?"

"I visited Kirby again. Offered him more money for more information. He seemed spooked. Told me to lose his address. Slammed the door in my face."

"Maybe I should go see him."

"No," Vince said in a firm tone.

"I could wear a disguise. Where does he live?" Andy had never shared that type of information with her. Mia had no idea where Andy met any of the men who hired him to commit a crime or those he searched out for information.

"Mia, I don't want you going anywhere around him. He had an arsenal laid out on his table. And there's something really sleazy about that guy."

"But he's one of my dad's friends."

Without responding, Vince went to the kitchen and returned with the wine bottle and filled their glasses.

Mia had no intention of allowing Vince to dictate who she could see and who she couldn't. She figured probably most of her father's friends were sleazy, but that didn't mean they'd harm her. As she sipped her wine, she pondered how she could find Kirby's address.

Mia's cell rang, startling both Vince and her. She picked it up and saw "unidentified caller" on the screen. Had she been alone she wouldn't have answered it, but with Vince sitting next to her, she pushed the answer button. "Hello."

"I liked the dress you wore today, but what I want is under it."

"Who is this?" she asked in a demanding tone.

The line went dead.

Mia turned to Vince. "Did you hear?"

He frowned. "Yes."

"What do you think?"

"From his voice, I'd guess he's middle-aged."

"I meant about what he said."

Vince gripped her hand. "I'm not sure if that's the guy who wants you dead. He sounds like he wants you in bed."

"A stalker? Nothing more?"

"Stalkers are dangerous too."

"Yes, but shooting first isn't normally a stalker's style. I can handle aggressive strangers provided they don't shoot or stab me before I even see them."

Vince gazed into her eyes and caressed her arm. "I

promise I won't let that happen to you."

Mia wasn't sure if he could keep that promise. Too many times she found herself alone—women's restroom, riding the elevator at work, and in her car. Everywhere she went now, she took her purse to keep her pistol within reach. Besides her place and Vince's, she felt she had to be constantly on guard, and she couldn't stay alert if she lacked sleep.

Mia ran her finger around the rim of her wine glass. "What's for dinner?"

"Roast chicken with red wine sauce." Vince headed to the kitchen and pulled the containers out of the fridge and dished up the salad.

As they sat down at the table, Vince's phone rang.

He glanced at the screen. His eyes narrowed, and his jaw became rigid. Then he turned it off. "Not important. And you had a late night. I want to make this an early one."

After everything had been cleaned up from dinner, they went down the hall toward her bedroom. Before they reached it, Vince pulled her into his arms and kissed her.

Mia gasped for breath. "Vince, we agreed to be associates, nothing more."

"That's what *you* wanted. I wanted more. I want this." He held her tighter and covered her lips with his.

She also wanted it but didn't want to mix business and pleasure. At least, not yet. Mia stretched out her hands to push him away, but then the tip of his tongue against her lips electrified her, sending a surge of excitement flaring through her body. Her heart raced, and her skin tingled with anticipation. She felt his warm breath and flushed with pleasure as he planted kisses down her neck. Her resolve completely vanished when he scooped her up into his arms and carried her to the bed.

Chapter 14

Mia had a hard time pulling herself away from the man who had given her such a memorable night. She would've liked nothing more than to stay curled up in his arms, but Andy's killer needed to be found first.

Gazing at Vince sleeping peacefully, she quietly eased into the bathroom. Mia stepped into the shower stall, and while she washed her hair, the shower door opened.

Vince softly trailed his fingers down her bare back and then swung her around, raised her chin, and kissed her. As he pulled her tight against his muscular chest, his kiss deepened.

Through ragged breaths, Mia said, "You keep this up, and I'll never make it to work."

"That's the point. Call in sick and stay with me."

"Vince, we still have a job to do—find a killer." She stared into his eyes and saw desire brimming in them. "I'd love to stay in bed with you, but it's unlikely we'll find the killer that way."

He gently touched her bruise. "Does this hurt?"

"No." Mia smiled. Several times during the night, he had been concerned if it was hurting her. "And stop worrying about it. I'll let you know if it starts bothering me."

He took the soap and began sudsing her chest. "Well, if you're determined to leave me, let me wash you first.

Forty-five minutes later, he dried her off.

"I'm definitely going to be late for work."

A mischievous smile flashed on his face. "Do you want me to write you an excuse?"

"Sure. Feinstein might get a good laugh out of that, but Lorraine sure won't."

He tilted his head. "Lorraine?"

"Yes. She's planning on inviting you to a party that one of her neighbors is throwing."

"Don't want to miss out on an invitation. I guess I'd better call her."

"Good idea. Do you intend to also share her bed?"

"You've spoiled me for any other woman."

"Doubt that."

He wrapped her in his arms, dropping the towel in the process, and kissed her. "Don't ever doubt that."

"We can finish this conversation later. Right now I need to get ready for work, and I can't do that while you're distracting me." Mia pointed to the door. "Out."

When Mia finished and stepped into the bedroom, she heard Vince on the phone in the living room but couldn't make out what he was saying. Thinking she might need a disguise if she somehow located Kirby's address, she emptied her duffle bag and put a strawberry-blonde wig, tight jeans, and a scoop-necked blouse in it. Since she didn't want Vince to catch wind of what she had in mind, she also put a foldable tote bag in it just in case he had planted another bug somewhere on the purse she intended to take to work. To cover up those items, she stuffed her jogging suit, a t-shirt, and athletic shoes on top of them.

She pulled out her cell phone, called the office, and asked Lorraine to tell Mr. Feinstein she had overslept and would be in soon.

"Good," Lorraine said. "He's been looking for you. Mr. Gunther is coming in later this morning."

Heading toward the living room, Mia thought about Gunther. She had always viewed him as a wealthy man, but according to Lorraine, he was having money problems, possibly losing his Mercedes dealerships. She couldn't imagine that would ever happen to the shady characters Andy dealt with. They'd plot out another heist and either handle it themselves or have their thugs do it or, if it required special expertise, hire it to be done.

As she continued mulling it over, Vince pointed to the duffle bag over her shoulder. "Why are you taking that?"

"I'm going to work out sometime today. There's a gym on the third floor. All of Feinstein's employees have a membership." She smiled at him. "And after last night and this morning, I need to stay in shape if I hope to keep up with you."

He rubbed her arm. "With your sore side, I think you could slack off a few days. And until we've determined who the killer is, it might not be safe to go there."

"I don't intend to work out vigorously. The place is always busy, and I'll make sure I'm never alone."

"Call me before you go there."

"Will do."

After he kissed her goodbye, Mia headed to the elevator.

* * *

When Mia reported to work, Lorraine told her that Feinstein wanted to see her in his office. She dropped off her duffle bag in her office and went to his.

"Good morning, Mia," Feinstein said in an upbeat tone. "Hank Gunther signed the contract yesterday. He is officially one of our clients."

"Great."

"He wants to see the presentation again before we put the commercial into production."

"Which one—Mercedes or BMW?"

"Both. Lewis and a technician are setting everything up in the conference room. I want you to be present in case...Lewis wants you to handle part of it."

"Certainly."

"Hank should be here in about twenty minutes."

Mia went back to her office to get the folder she had put together on the Gunther presentations and then headed to the conference room.

"Hey, Lewis," she greeted him.

"Good morning, Mia," he said coldly without looking at her as he fiddled with his computer.

Something was still amiss with Lewis.

Before she had a chance to talk to him about it, Gunther and Feinstein showed up.

"Hello, Mia," Gunther said, moving around the table toward her. "Can I talk to you privately?"

Mia glanced at Feinstein.

He nodded.

She stepped out into the hallway with Gunther.

"I missed having a drink with you after the fundraiser. I understand you went home sick. How are you feeling now?"

"Fine. It was just something I ate that didn't agree with me."

"Would you consider going with me to the Business Owners of the Year Award Banquet? I'm receiving an award."

Mia forced a smile. "Congratulations, Hank. What night is the banquet?"

"Thursday night. I had intended to ask you earlier, but there was a chance that I wouldn't be able to attend."

"I already have an engagement that night, but let me see if I can get out of it. Would it be okay to let you know tomorrow?" Going with him was nothing Mia wanted to do, but she also didn't want to turn him down if there was a chance he was or had hired Andy's killer. And since it appeared his financial problems were cleared up, she was suspicious.

"Tomorrow will be fine." Gunther pulled out a business card and wrote on it. "That's my cell phone number."

Mia took the card. When she returned to her seat, she put it in her purse.

After both mock commercials, Lewis and Mia left the conference room. In the hallway, she said, "Lewis, you did another nice job. Gunther was engrossed."

"At least he didn't spend most of his time watching you." Lewis had an edge in his voice.

Ignoring Lewis's remark, Mia turned on her heel

and went to her office, feeling irritated.

Mia spent the following hour searching the internet for Brayton Kirby. A few people popped up with that name, but after a lot of clicking, it became obvious that none of them were the Brayton Kirby she sought. Then she wondered if there was any possibility that Andy had phone numbers hidden somewhere. He never left anything to do with their business in his apartment. He had no intention of making the same mistake their Dad had made. He'd say, "Let the cops and thugs search every inch of my place. They'll never find anything because there won't be anything to find."

Once, after Andy had bought the auto repair shop, he wanted Mia to see it. She dressed up in one of her disguises, and he took her there. She smiled, remembering how excited her brother was to show it off. Besides locks on the doors, the shop had no special security equipment that might draw unwanted attention. Mia knew if her brother had anything to hide, like phone numbers, that's where she would find it. She also knew that Andy had an accountant who was in charge when Andy wasn't there. Since Andy's auto mechanic business had been thriving, she figured the accountant would keep things functioning, at least for a while.

Shortly after lunch, Mia's cell phone rang. Wondering if it was Vince, she pulled it out of her purse and saw the call came from the police department. "Hello," she answered.

"Is this Mia Sloan?"

"Yes."

"This is Lieutenant Collins. I'm investigating a burglary at Oliver LeMonte's home. I have a few questions for you regarding your visit there last Wednesday night and your stay on Sunday night. Would you rather discuss that at your office, or would you prefer to come here?"

"I'd rather go there."

"Can you make it after work?"

"Yes."

Lieutenant Collins gave her the address and then ended the call.

As Mia ran everything over in her mind that she intended to tell the Lieutenant about both visits, someone knocked on her door.

"Yes," she said loudly.

"Mia, it's Lewis."

"Come on in."

Lewis entered and closed the door behind him, which was unusual. He moved a chair closer to her desk and sat down. "Mia, I just can't take it anymore. I couldn't sleep last night."

Mia stared at him. "Lewis, what's this about?"

"You need to return the ring. I've been thinking it over, and I can't figure out what in the world possessed you to steal it."

Mia gazed at the ring on her finger. "Lewis, is that why you've been avoiding me? Because you thought I stole the ring?"

Lewis reached out and placed his hand on top of hers. "Mia, after you told me the story of how you acquired it, I called LeMonte, attempting to get you a better discount on it. Since I believed the ring wasn't completely paid for—you told me your aunt gave you a good down payment, not the entire price—there was a chance I could get them to credit your account with an additional discount. Over the years, I've done a lot of business with LeMonte."

"Lewis, LeMonte's is an expensive store. How have you managed to do a lot of business with them?"

"I'm not here to discuss my situation, but I will tell you all of my transactions with them have been fully paid, unlike the ring you're wearing. LeMonte has no copy of a purchase receipt or an account for Mia Sloan."

"That's confidential information, Lewis."

"I'm a highly regarded customer, and since my goal was to benefit you, not to find out if you owed them money, I was able to obtain information from Marilyn Garrett who manages the store when LeMonte is away. And during that conversation, I also found out that Oliver was out of town when you claimed he allowed you to borrow that ring. Mia, this is so out of character for you to steal a ring. Please explain it to me."

"Lewis, I didn't steal it. When I went to the store, I dealt with a man who was very knowledgeable about precious stones. I assumed he was Oliver LeMonte. It wasn't until the fundraiser that I discovered the man was actually Vince Tolbert, Oliver's cousin. He was the man who allowed me to take the ring and determine if I wanted to buy it. As I told you, I returned the ring. I also dealt with him when I purchased it. Why don't you call the store and talk to him?"

Lewis whipped out his cell phone and placed the call.

Not what Mia had expected. She thought suggesting it would be enough to sway Lewis that she hadn't lied about that.

Lewis stood and moved away from her. "May I speak to Vince Tolbert?...Do you know when he'll be in the store?...Thank you." He swung around and faced her. "Vince hasn't been in the store since Tuesday. When he's in town, he sometimes drops by, but nothing routine. Mia, LeMonte's house was recently robbed. The exact date hasn't been determined since Oliver has been out of town for two weeks."

"But Vince is staying there."

"How do you know that?"

"He told me."

"Whether he is staying there or not, that wouldn't point to a specific day for the robbery. Oliver is the only one who knows the combination to the safe that was robbed. I've heard diamonds were taken, but also while Oliver was gone, someone broke into the safe at the store. If anyone recognizes that you are wearing a LeMonte ring, like I did, you could easily become a person of interest. If I were you, I would return it to the store and make up some kind of excuse how it came into your possession. But Mia, don't say a family member gave it to you. That story won't hold up."

"Honestly, Lewis, I didn't steal it. I'm going to try to reach Vince Tolbert. I'm sure he can clear this whole thing up."

"For your sake, I sure hope so." Lewis stared at Mia for a minute and then turned and walked out of her office, closing the door behind him.

Mia briefly closed her eyes. *Vince has set me up. He knew where the safe was located but not the combination. He needed me to crack it so he could get the diamonds. No wonder he wanted me to wear the ring. He knew the police would want to talk to me. Seeing that ring on my finger might land me in jail. It'll be my word against Vince Tolbert, who has part ownership of LeMonte's Fine Jewelry. No one will believe me. Obviously, Lewis didn't.*

Rubbing her forehead, she wondered how she could've been so easily played. Sadness came over her. She had fallen for the guy and believed he truly cared for her. Vince had seemed overprotective. He took care of her when she was at the farm, mourning Andy's death. *How could I have gotten it so wrong?* She thought about the surveillance cameras Vince had claimed were off. Wandering through the house that night, she had glanced at them and they appeared off, not even a small light occasionally flickered from them in the dark. Still, she worried that he had a recording showing her cracking the safe. During all the times she worked with Andy, Mia always hid her face under a ski mask. But since she had trusted Vince, she had assumed that wasn't necessary. After all, she didn't believe it was a real robbery. And to make matters worse, she had left Vince in her apartment where the stethoscope was in a drawer. One more piece of evidence against her.

Mia ran her fingers through her hair, trying to grasp how she could deal with this betrayal. An idea popped into her mind. She gripped her purse, headed to the restroom, went into the handicap stall, and removed her dress. Mia turned her cell phone camera on and began taking pictures of the large bruise on her side. With a devious smile on her face, she put her dress on and headed back to her office. Sitting at her desk, she downloaded the photos to her computer and sent them to her personal email.

Then she took an advertising book off of her shelf, removed the ring and securely taped it to the exterior of the pages. She replaced the book and quickly pulled it out to make sure the ring would remain in place if someone wanted to check the shelf behind the books. Mia realized that wasn't a great spot to hide the ring, but she wanted to keep it safe so she could throw it at Vince someday.

Before she went to the police department, Mia wanted to search for her brother's killer just in case the scheduled interview took a bad turn. She had no intention of running and hoped her plan might get her off the hook. Still, she knew it would be long and drawn out, and by then, any tracks to Andy's killer might be gone.

Mia picked up the phone and placed a call to Lieutenant Collins. After he greeted her, she said, "When I made the appointment to go to your office after work, I completely forgot about another engagement. Could I reschedule for tomorrow after work?"

"Let me see…would tomorrow at 6:30 p.m. work for you?"

"Yes. Perfect. Thank you."

With that problem delayed, Mia devised a plan to leave Feinstein's without being noticed by either Vince's men or anyone else who had an interest in her whereabouts.

When it was an hour before quitting time, Mia pulled the folded tote out of her duffle bag and moved the needed contents from her purse, checking each item for bugs. She put the almost empty purse into her bottom file cabinet drawer and her cell phone into her top desk drawer.

Mia went out to the receptionist's desk. "Lorraine. My aunt isn't feeling well, so I'm going to leave a little early. If Mr. Feinstein comes looking for me, can you tell him?"

"Sure. Your poor aunt. Hope she gets better soon."

"Thanks. See you tomorrow."

Mia took the elevator down to the second floor. Then she went into that floor's women's restroom and into the handicap stall. There, she changed into a disguise—strawberry blonde wig, tight jeans, and a scoop-necked blouse—she had intended to wear to visit Kirby if and when she located his address.

After she checked herself out in the mirror and put on a heavy coat of makeup, Mia walked down the stairs to the lobby, left the building, and headed to the subway.

Chapter 15

Mia rode the subway for three stops and then switched to another subway line. When she was within two miles of Andy's shop, an area of town where she had noticed several rundown motels, she headed to one that looked like it was in serious need of maintenance.

Tipping the clerk at the front desk $100, she rented a room for cash under the name Jane Smith. No ID needed. The room was much nicer and cleaner than she had anticipated. Mia left her duffle bag in the room and headed out the door.

When she checked in, she had asked the clerk for directions to the closest fast food place. Carrying her tote, she followed his instructions and passed a row of stores on the way. Hoping she could find a ski mask in one of them, she sauntered in and out of several. At the back of the third store she saw a bin full of miscellaneous winter items—gloves, scarves, hats—on sale. Mia rummaged through it and, near the bottom, found a ski mask.

Paying for it, she asked the sales clerk, "Is there a drug store nearby?"

"A block away." The clerk pointed that direction.

"Thanks."

After making her second purchase, Mia bought a hamburger and fries and returned to the motel.

Feeling good that she had everything she needed for her planned visit to Andy's shop, she took off her wig and ate. While she waited for the sun to set, she stretched out on the bed and thought about Vince. *Does he think I've been nabbed by the culprit? Murdered? Or does he suspect I caught onto his scheme and took off?* At least Mia knew that once he left her apartment, he couldn't return. She was counting on the concierge to handle that.

Shortly before 9:00 p.m., Mia put on her black jogging suit and athletic shoes. She stuck the ski mask and latex gloves into her tote bag and began her hike to the shop her brother had been so proud of.

About a hundred feet away from it, she saw lights on at each corner of the building and over the doors but no surveillance cameras. The area around the building was industrial and quiet. No one was in sight. Still, as a precaution, she reached into her tote and pulled out the ski mask and slipped it on. Staying on high alert, she made her way to the shop's side entrance, lifted out her small flashlight, and turned it on. She tugged on the latex gloves and picked the padlock and then the lock in the doorknob. She quickly stepped inside, locked the door behind her, and placed the padlock on the floor.

Mia gazed around. Two cars were raised on hydraulic racks. She wandered over to the counters and glanced at the tools spread over them. Nothing unusual. Mia went into the office near the side door and began going through the drawers. Then she immediately stopped. *Andy was clever at hiding things. He'd never put anything important in a place where it could be easily found, unless he wanted it found.* Mia surveyed the office. She ran her gloved fingers over and under the desk, searching for hidden compartments. Then she figured any information about their heists wouldn't be found in the office—too obvious. Mia scanned the shop again. She bent down and looked in the well below the cars on the hydraulic lifts. Nothing appeared out of the ordinary.

Heavy cardboard boxes stood on one side of the room. She looked through them—new tools and car parts. Mia felt under the shelves and checked the wall behind tool racks. As her eyes drifted around the place, she sensed something was hidden, almost as if Andy were guiding her. She continued searching every nook and cranny. Just when Mia was about to give up she noticed the electric box on the wall. The panel-board cover seemed oversized. She opened the door in it. The switches lined up. *Why is the panel board around the door so big?*

Wanting to check it out further, Mia took a Phillips screwdriver off of a rack, unscrewed the panel board cover and lowered it to the floor. Under the wires sat a five-by-eight metal box about two inches deep.

Mia pulled it out and, before she looked at the contents, secured the panel cover back in place and returned the screwdriver to the rack. She was just about to open the metal box when she heard a diesel engine. Light appeared around the bay doors. She assumed a truck had stopped in front of the shop.

Mia shoved the box into her tote and, recalling there was a back window in the office, hurried to that room, closing the door behind her. She flipped off her flashlight and dropped it in her tote as she heard the side door creak open.

"Hey, what's the padlock doing on the floor?" a husky voice said.

"No cars outside. Check the office." That voice was deep and equally gruff.

Mia dived into the knee hole of the desk and pulled her tote against her. She had been in tight spots before, but this was the first time that Andy wasn't nearby to help her. Mia's heart beat frantically while a cold chill swept through her body. She wanted to rummage through her tote bag for her weapon but didn't dare make a sound.

The door flew open. "No one in here. Want me to search the office again?"

"No. We've already looked through everything in there. Still can't understand that guy not having one photo in his apartment. How can anyone not have at least one? That red Corvette hasn't budged since we were here before. We didn't search the cars in the shop last time. Start with that. I'm calling the boss about the padlock."

Footsteps pounded on the cement floor, and then a door squeaked.

Mia edged out of the knee hole, peered around the edge of the desk, and saw the office door stood ajar. Figuring the boss, whoever he was, might send more guys when he learned about the padlock, she couldn't stick around and wait for those two guys to finish searching the shop. She knew the Corvette was in the bay farthest away from the office. Avoiding being seen through the small door opening, she inched to the window and slowly raised the blinds. Then she unlatched the lock and attempted to lift the window, but it wouldn't budge.

Wondering what could be used to pry it open, she crept back to the desk and stealthily opened the top drawer. Near a tray that held pens and pencils were a few utensils. She grabbed a knife and forced it under the window. Using all her strength, the window slowly rose. Listening to the scrapping sound it caused, Mia held her breath, hoping the noise had gone undetected. Since the window was her only escape route, she had to keep forcing it up until it was high enough for her to squeeze out. Not hearing footsteps moving in her direction, Mia pushed her tote through the opening and then wiggled out.

Car tires screeched on the nearby pavement.

Fearing she might be seen from the street, Mia decided not to run to the closest industrial, metal building. She dropped to the ground and crawled to it.

Staying in the shadows, she stood and looked around the corner of the metal building and saw a black SUV with headlights on next to a Ford truck in front of Andy's shop.

An angry voice erupted inside. "The window! You never checked! Find him. Now!"

Convinced he was talking about her. Mia's pulse quickened and her adrenaline spiked as she sprinted away, scrambling over a few chain-link fences, and meandering around dumpsters, large pieces of equipment, parked semi-trucks, and other industrial buildings while she heard engines roaring and banging and clanking noises behind her.

When she had gone several blocks, Mia removed the ski mask, gloves, and the top of her jogging suit, revealing a colorful t-shirt underneath. She stuck those items in her tote and continued moving along. Spotting a few people on the sidewalk in front of a bar, she stepped out of the shadows. Her breathing returned to normal and her heartbeat slowed down. She felt safe.

Back in her motel room, she pulled the metal box out of her tote. Staring at it, Mia exhaled and inhaled deeply. Within a minute, she had picked the lock and was looking at the contents. On top was a sheet from a yellow notepad. She unfolded it. The note on it read:

> *Sis,*
>
> *Guess I didn't make it if you're reading this. That wood box should have stayed buried. Thought it might be a treasure. I screwed up telling the wrong person. Mom and Aunt Thelma had a good reason for helping bury it. Don't trust J.D. or Kirby. One of them believes you know what was in it. That guy will do anything to keep the contents a secret. You've got to kill 'em or clear out.*
>
> *I always loved you. Andy*
>
> *P.S. The ring. J.D. gave it to me a few years back. Said it was a bonus for a heist. But something about it didn't smell right. Never wore it. Looks expensive. Guess that's why I kept it.*

Mia's lips trembled and her eyes moistened, but she was determined to keep her emotions in check. She went into the bathroom and wiped her eyes.

Then she proceeded to look at the other items in the box. She lifted out a stack of pictures and the ring.

Gazing at the size of the diamond encased in a gold band with intricate carvings on it, she had no doubt her brother was right—it was expensive. Even though Andy had apprehensions about it, maybe he planned to hawk it to get some of the money to pay off J.D. Mia smiled, thinking that would've been a strange twist—J.D. gave Andy the ring, and Andy used it to pay off a debt owed to J.D.

Mia squinted when she looked at the first picture. On it was her mother and a man she didn't recognize. He had light brown hair and blue eyes like hers. His arm was around her mother. They were smiling. Mia thought her mom looked happy. Wondering who the man was, Mia flipped it over and saw a year had been written on it—the same year Mia turned ten and the same year the box had been buried. Mia recalled her mother going on trips by herself, claiming they were farm co-op trips. When Mia became older, she realized they couldn't have been legitimate since Aunt Thelma owned the farm, and her mother never made any decisions about its operation. But when her mother returned from those trips, her face always glowed, and she sang along with all the tunes on the radio. Mia had often wondered if her mother had taken off to spend time with her father. Gazing at the picture, Mia suddenly doubted that.

She went to the next picture. A man held a gun over another man lying on a cement floor in a pool of blood. The man on the floor—his face was clearly visible—was unfamiliar to her. It only showed a side view of the armed man's face. Staring at the profile, she thought she had seen him before but wasn't certain. Since the pictures had been taken over twenty years earlier, she knew he wouldn't look exactly the same.

Mia continued going through the photos. On most of them, several men held guns and bloody men's and a few women's bodies were on the floor. It appeared to her that a mass shooting had taken place. *Why was Mom there?* With the exception of the man holding a gun in the second picture, none of the others looked even remotely familiar, but like the gunman in the second picture, they all would have aged.

Putting the pictures back in the metal box, she suspected they were probably what got Andy killed. She guessed he had made inquiries about the people in them. Like Andy said in his note, he told "the wrong person." *And either J.D. or Kirby believes I know the contents of the box.* Mia figured that was why Andy had been so concerned about her safety.

After she closed the lid, Mia wondered what had happened to the other contents of the footlocker-sized wooden box. *Could Andy have given it to someone? Maybe the culprit? Thinking it would get him off the hook?*

Mia considered who would kill for the pictures. *Maybe a relative or associate of the dead people is still searching for the killers, as Vince is for his cousin's killer. And maybe Andy's killer feared that person. Could that be it?* Andy's note said that either J.D. or Kirby would do anything to keep the box's contents a secret. *Why didn't Mom and Aunt Thelma just burn it?* That certainly would've prevented it from ever resurfacing. Mia tapped her fingers together. *Could they have kept it for some kind of insurance?* Mom had been there. *Maybe someone threatened exposing the contents if anything happened to her.*

Whatever the reason, Mia vowed to solve the

mystery. Before seeking out J.D.'s identity, she planned to try to find out the names of at least some of the victims in the photos and intended to start by looking through newspaper archives for murdered or missing people around that time.

Anxious to begin her quest, she used the motel telephone and called for a **taxi.**

Chapter 16

It was 2:16 a.m. when the taxi driver pulled over to the curb in front of Mia's apartment building. She paid him and hurried inside.

Standing in the lobby was Owen, one of Vince's men. "Mia," he said, sounding relieved and pulling out his cell phone. "We've been searching everywhere for you." Owen pushed a button on his phone.

"If you're calling Vince, tell him I don't want to see him again."

Owen's eyes narrowed in confusion as Mia headed to the bank of elevators.

"But Mia..."

She turned toward him. "No buts. I don't want to see him, and that's final."

"I've got your stuff," Owen said, moving toward her with a bag

Mia took it from him. "Thanks." She noticed the concierge eyeing Owen and guessed he'd stop Owen if he attempted to follow her.

After getting off the elevator, Mia walked toward

her apartment and saw a large vase filled with red roses outside her door. She stepped around them, unlocked her door, and put everything she was carrying inside. Then she picked up the vase and put it on her kitchen counter.

She assumed they were from Vince and wondered how he intended to justify his actions. Mia lifted the card. It read, "Mia, you are the best thing that has happened to me for a long time, Vince."

What did he mean by "for a long time"? His long time might only be a week, maybe less. Whatever he meant by it didn't matter to Mia. She had no intention of letting him back into her life. Still, the roses were beautiful, so she moved the vase to her dining room table to enjoy.

Mia opened the bag Owen had given her and pulled out her cell phone and the purse she had left at work. Not seeing the ring she had hidden, Mia smiled. Then she checked her phone. There were five voice messages from Vince received between 5:10 p.m. and 7:00 p.m. She assumed no messages came after that because either Vince or one of his men had broken into her office, looking for clues to her whereabouts. Mia tapped on the messages. In each one, Vince wanted to know where she was. His voice sounded desperate in the last message.

Mia shook her head and said out loud, "Vince, you are good. Had I not discovered the truth, I would've believed you truly are concerned about my well-being. I'm not going down that road again. Goodbye, Vince Tolbert." Mia just hoped she could manage to stay out of jail, at least long to find Andy's killer.

While she still held her cell phone, it rang, and Vince's name appeared on the screen. Mia turned it off, moved the metal box to her bedroom, and got ready for bed.

* * *

Mia awoke when her alarm went off at 8:30 a.m. She hadn't planned to go to work but intended to call in. She turned on her phone and saw three more messages from Vince. Ignoring them, she placed the call.

"Hi, Lorraine." Mia's voice dragged. "This is Mia."

"Oh, Mia, you don't sound well."

"I'm not. I've been up most of the night, taking care of my aunt. I probably caught her bug."

"I'll tell Mr. Feinstein you won't be in. Try to get some sleep. Drink chicken broth and plenty of water. That always helps."

"Thanks. Maybe I'll see you tomorrow."

With that task done, Mia used the camera on her cell phone and snapped a photo of each picture Andy had hidden. She searched her bedroom for a secure hiding spot to put the photos, but no place seemed right. She went into the kitchen to look around. Mia used her mini screwdriver to remove the bottom of her coffee maker, and stuck the photos in it. Once it was screwed back together, she doubted the photos would ever be found if she were nabbed or killed.

After a quick breakfast, Mia dressed in jeans and a sweater. Just in case something came up, she emptied her duffle bag and put another disguise in it. She slipped Andy's note in her tote bag and stuck the man's ring in her jewelry box. She placed the empty metal box on a shelf in her closet.

Mia's cell phone rang. She waited for the ringing to

stop, and then picked it up. Like she had guessed, the missed call was from Vince. She clicked on her Uber app and ordered a ride to the New York Library on Fifth Avenue.

She flung the strap of her duffle bag over her shoulder, picked up her tote, and went to the elevator. Mia worried that Vince or one of his men would be in the lobby or right outside the door, but she figured, even if she exited by the parking garage, they'd be close by. And she also assumed Vince would want to keep her safe in order to pin the diamond theft on her.

Only the concierge was in the lobby as Mia walked to the entrance. He opened the door for her. She thanked him and then climbed into the waiting Uber car.

After she was dropped off at the library, Mia went straight to the research section and began tapping on a computer. It didn't take her long to click into the newspaper archive files and start her search for people murdered or missing the same year the box was buried.

"What are you looking for?" Vince stood behind her.

"Well, not you." Mia kept her eyes on the computer.

He pulled up a chair next to her and sat down. "Mia, what have I done?"

Mia turned to him. "Come on, Vince. Did you honestly not think I would catch on?"

"Catch on to what?"

"Being played." She whispered, "You needed me to open that safe because you didn't know the combo, and then you asked me to wear a ring that you would claim was stolen. You probably expect me to be arrested the minute Lieutenant Collins sees that ring on my finger."

"Mia, I didn't..."

She held up her hand. "Stop. I have work to do, and I'd appreciate it if you'd leave me to it. Once I'm locked up, you can come and visit me there and tell me how terribly sorry you are. Probably telling me you had nothing to do with it. It was completely out of your control. Something like that."

A librarian moved toward them.

"Now go before I get kicked out."

"No. I won't leave you like this."

Mia didn't trust Vince but doubted she could easily get rid of him. Since the identities of the people she was seeking had nothing to do with the theft of diamonds, she figured she might as well put him to work.

"Okay. If you're going to hang around, sit at that computer." She gestured toward the next one in the row. She brought up one of the pictures on her cell phone, the one with the shooter who looked vaguely familiar. "Go to newspaper archives around twenty-one years ago and search for murdered and missing people. You're looking for this guy." Mia pointed to the dead guy in the photo.

Vince's eyes opened wider. "You don't know who this is?"

Mia shook her head.

Vince stood and took Mia's arm. "Grab your stuff. We need to get out of here."

"But..."

"Now," he ordered.

Vince obviously knows the identity of the man. Mia

147

clicked out of newspaper archives and picked up her tote and duffle bag.

Vince led her to his Alfa Romeo. When they were strapped in, he pulled out his phone and pushed a button. "Owen, I need an escort to my house."

"Be there in six minutes."

As he disconnected, Mia asked, "Why? I might be angry with you, but I hadn't planned to shoot you…however tempting that might be."

"Mia, the dead guy in that photo is Luca Russo."

Mia's mouth fell open. She had never seen a picture of the nefarious crime boss's son, but she had heard the name. Her father had sometimes talked about the Russo family. The crime boss, Morellus Russo, and his hoodlums terrorized sections of the city. Just speaking his name sent chills up the spines of store owners in certain areas of *his* town. They paid a fee for protection or else they were never seen again. The family was also into gambling, prostitution, and who knew what else. Morrellus Russo paid a fortune to investigators and thugs to find his missing son. Morellus also paid informants, but rumor had it that informants were swiftly terminated when their information led to a dead end. It was believed Luca had been murdered and his body buried someplace. Nothing surfaced to prove that, but the hunt changed from finding his son to finding his son's killer. More money crossed palms, and more people died.

Vince explained more. "About eight years ago, Morellus Russo turned the control of his criminal empire over to his second son, Lorenzo, who vowed to continue the search for his brother's killer. And once the assassin or assassins are found, the word is that they will be tortured, quartered, and pieces of their bodies spread through the neighborhoods where they did business. Furthermore, all of their family members will be slaughtered. Everyone knows Lorenzo doesn't make idle threats.

"The police tried for years to find solid evidence against Morellus Russo, but he never got his hands dirty. He paid well for others to do his bidding, and no one ever dared speak against him. At least, not where it could be overheard. Lorenzo is following in his father's footsteps."

One question ran through Mia's mind. *Who is the dumb schmuck holding the gun?*

"Mia, where did you get the picture?"

Since no photos remained in that spot, and even though she didn't trust Vince, she saw no harm in telling him the truth. "I found it and others well-hidden in my brother's shop."

"They must have been. Those pictures probably got Andy killed. Most likely, the killer is hunting for them right now."

"Some thugs came to the shop while I was there. I hid in the office and overheard them talking. One guy mentioned not finding any pictures in Andy's apartment. From what they said, that was the second time they came to search the shop."

"How did you get out of there?"

"Through the office window."

A black BMW with heavily tinted windows pulled into the next parking stall. Owen stepped out of it. As he came closer, Vince rolled down his window.

"Owen, I need to talk to Mia for a minute." Vince watched Owen climb back into the BMW, and then turned to Mia. "Do you have the pictures with you?"

"No. They're in a safe place."

"Mia, the person searching for those pictures knows your true identity—that you're Andy Carlyle's sister, his partner in crime. Most likely, they've already thoroughly searched Andy's apartment. When they can't find the pictures in his shop, they'll show up at your apartment. There's no place safe there, and no building is secure enough to keep out professional thugs. They could be holding off making a serious move on you because the man in charge might not be certain that you're aware of the photos. That uncertainty will be ripped away if even one of those pictures is found in your apartment, and every inch of it will be searched including vents and everything that can be taken apart. I suspect the culprit responsible for your brother's death and my cousin's is in one of those pictures." Vince studied Mia's face. "I want to keep you safe, but I can't do that if you refuse to let me. Can we go and get those pictures, or would you rather take your chances?"

Mia still doubted Vince was trustworthy, but finding her brother's killer was her top priority. She needed to stay alive in order to do that. Even though she didn't want to accept any help from Vince, she couldn't think of another option.

"Mia?"

"The pictures are in my apartment. Take me there, and I'll get them."

Vince got out of the car and tapped on Owen's window. "We'll be making a stop at Mia's place on the way to my home." He climbed back into the driver's seat and pulled out of the parking lot with Owen about a car length behind him.

As they drove, Mia replayed Andy's note in her head. According to it, the culprit already believed she knew the secrets the box contained. With the exception of the guy trying to grab her one night, no one had come after her. The killer probably was holding off until all the places Andy could've hidden the pictures had been exhausted. *Vince is probably right. I'm not safe at home, and neither are the pictures.*

Vince stopped by the curb near the front of her building. Since there wasn't a free spot close to him, Owen ended up parking in a red zone.

Owen stayed outside while Mia and Vince went into the apartment building. When they reached her unit, she hurried into her bedroom and grabbed her mini screwdriver. It didn't take her long to remove the pictures from the coffee maker. She handed them to Vince. "Hold these while I get the metal box."

She headed to her closet and retrieved the box. Then she pulled out a suitcase and began filling it with enough clothing to last her a week. Thinking she didn't want anyone snooping around to run into the stethoscope and wigs, she stuck them into the suitcase.

Mia looked around, wanting to make sure there wasn't anything left that could tie her to any crime. Her eyes stopped on her jewelry box. Recalling the man's ring, she pulled it out of the box and glanced over the other jewelry. She had nothing expensive, but there were some sentimental pieces she got from her mother. On that thought, she put her jewelry box in the suitcase and gave Vince the ring. "This was also in the metal box."

Vince stared at the ring. "Do you know where your brother got this?"

"He mentions it in his note."

"What note?"

"It was in the box. I'll let you read it at your place."

Vince helped her close her suitcase. "Do you really need to take all this stuff?"

"Yes." Mia took the pictures and ring from Vince, put them in the metal box, and slipped it into her purse. "Ready."

Chapter 17

Walking into Vince's place, Mia said, "I had completely forgotten Oliver was in town. Will he be okay with me staying here for a few days?"

"Mia, this is just as much my house as it is his. I don't need to ask his permission to have a house guest, but he'll be fine with it." A goofy grin flashed on his face.

"What?"

"I'll tell you during lunch."

Mia looked over her shoulder and saw the dining table was set for two. "When did you call?"

"When you were busy filling your suitcase. I'm going to take it upstairs."

"I'll come with you. I want to freshen up."

Vince headed straight to his room.

"Hey. Hey. Not in there. I want to stay in one of the guest rooms."

Vince gazed at her for a minute, turned, and went into the closest guest room. Putting down the suitcase, he asked, "What can I do to fix this?"

"Lewis is convinced I stole the ring you gave me to wear."

Vince lowered his eyes. "Lewis. Why?"

Mia explained why Lewis thought she had stolen it and then said, "I want a store receipt, showing that I bought the ring. Leave a little balance for an amount still due."

"Where is the ring?"

"At work. It's safe. After chatting with Lewis, I had no intention on parading around with it on my finger, especially to the police department. By the way, I have an appointment today at 6:30 with Lieutenant Collins."

"I'll take you."

"Why? So you can hand over the recording showing me breaking into the safe?"

"Mia, I put the surveillance cameras out of commission that night. Don't you believe me?"

"No, I don't. You also inferred you could open that safe, but only Oliver knows the combination. How do you explain that?"

Vince sat down on the edge of the bed and took Mia's hand. "Sit by me."

She waved her free hand. "No funny business?"

"No funny business."

Mia eased down by him.

"I had planned to use you. I've already told you I have recordings of conversations you had with your brother. I expected you to play a role in helping me find Ethan's killer. What I didn't expect was to find you the most intriguing woman I've ever met."

"And how is that?" *He just can't stop trying to play me.*

"Besides being gorgeous, you are exceptionally skilled at hiding your criminal side. And your smile. I was completely hooked the first time we dined on the balcony. And then at the farm, I discovered your gentle, soft side and wanted nothing more than to protect you." He tucked a loose strand of hair behind her ear. "Also, you are the only woman I've ever been with who would understand the dark world, danger, and adrenaline rush I sometimes experience in investigating a crime for a client.

"After the time we spent together at your apartment, I thought you trusted me, but then you snuck away from work so my men couldn't follow you. You didn't answer my calls and told Owen you never wanted to see me again. Why didn't you call me after Lewis talked to you?"

"Vince, you still haven't explained the safe business."

He caressed her arm. "I don't know the combination, but, if you will recall, I had intended to claim the uncut diamonds had been stolen. You were the one who wanted to actually stage the heist."

Mia felt the color drain from her face. *He's right. It was me. Why did I jump to the worst conclusion when Lewis told me only Oliver knew the combination?*

Vince put his arms around her. "Mia, it's okay. You were mourning your brother when we talked about it. Details can get cloudy."

"It's probably because I'm used to playing a mark. I know how it works. I guess I assumed…"

"Hey." Vince raised her chin. "Don't worry about it." He softly kissed her lips and smiled. "Are we good now?"

"As soon as you write me a receipt for the ring. When Lewis left my office yesterday, he acted like I was the scum of the earth, stealing from LeMonte's. I have to prove to him I'm not a thief."

Vince and Mia laughed at the irony.

"I'll take care of the receipt after lunch."

"Had I not broken into the safe and taken the diamonds, would Oliver have gone along with claiming the diamonds had been stolen?"

"He would've been a hard sell. Oliver has difficulty lying, but he's anxious to find his brother's killer. I think I could've swayed him." Vince ran his fingertips down Mia's cheek. "You made that easier. Oliver doesn't know it wasn't a real heist."

While they ate, Mia asked, "What did you find so funny after you told me Oliver would be okay with me staying here?"

"Lorraine called last night. She wanted to update me about what was going on at Feinstein's and mentioned you left early because her aunt was sick again. She felt really bad about your aunt." He took a sip of water. "Until she called, I thought you had been nabbed by the person or persons behind Andy's death."

"Lorraine likes to talk. She has a tough time keeping anything quiet." Mia squinted. "But I'm afraid I don't see what's funny about that."

"That isn't the amusing part of the conversation I had with Lorraine. She asked me to go with her to a party at her neighbors... like you told me she would."

"What's funny about that?"

"Oliver's wife divorced him last year. She's a stern, moody woman. We never got along, but for Oliver's sake I tried to be pleasant around her. The truth be known, Oliver almost seemed relieved that she divorced him. Rumor has it that she took him to the cleaners. Not true. He had a pre-nup. That's beside the point. Since I couldn't make it to Lorraine's neighbor's party, she's taking Oliver."

"How did you arrange that?"

"I mentioned he was feeling down and could use a night out. Lorraine immediately jumped on the opportunity to cheer him up. Oliver had already met Lorraine at a party Feinstein threw, so I knew he'd be conducive to the idea. He's picking her up Saturday at 7:30."

"Wow. I can hardly wait to see what Lorraine tells me tomorrow. I'm sure by now the whole office knows she's going out with Oliver LeMonte."

After lunch, Vince headed to the den to print a receipt, and Mia went upstairs to get her purse with the metal box in it.

As she entered the den, Vince handed her the receipt.

Mia gazed at it. "This looks so real." Her eyes moved to Vince. "Is this legal? Do I owe that much money to LeMonte's?"

"Yes," Vince said with a stern expression on his face. "But I did give you an appreciably larger discount than Lewis could've arranged."

Mia laughed. "Isn't that sweet of you. By the way, do you know how Lewis affords the jewelry he buys?"

"Have you heard of the Gasner Foundation?"

"Yes."

"Lewis's mother is the benefactor."

"Lewis's mother?"

"Yes. She's an only child and inherited a fortune when her parents died."

"You gave me the impression that Lewis might be a suspect."

"His mother controls the purse strings in that family. She probably dishes out money to him sometimes, but she calls all the shots. Most men wouldn't like that. Regardless of how he acted about the ring, don't eliminate the possibility that he could be involved."

"I won't." Mia put the metal box on the desk and took out the contents.

The color drained from Vince's face as he lifted up the man's ring. "This belonged to Ethan."

Mia caressed Vince's arm. "I'm so sorry. Andy never wore it. Read his note." She gave him the folded page and watched him read it.

"It appears J.D. killed Ethan, but he might not be responsible for Andy's death."

"That's how I see it too. Andy said that either J.D. or Kirby knew my true identity, and one of them would do anything to keep the box contents a secret. Maybe one of them is in these photos. That would explain why he'd kill to keep the pictures hidden." Mia held up a picture. "That's my mom next to that man."

"That's your mom?" Vince said with a puzzled expression on his face. "The guy with his arm around her is Lorenzo Russo."

"Are you sure?"

Vince nodded. "He's younger in the picture, but that's definitely him."

"Do you think he had his brother knocked off?"

Vince shrugged as he flipped through the pictures. "It sure looks like he was at the same place where his brother was killed, so my guess would be yes. Didn't your mother live with you at the farm?"

"Yes, she did, but she often took what she called

'farm co-op trips'."

"Looks like she hung around with a rough crowd."

Mia held the picture that showed Luca's body on the floor and pointed to the gunman. "Something about him seems familiar. Any idea who he is?"

Vince shook his head as he examined the other photos. "Besides Lorenzo and Luca, I don't recognize any of the others. I suspect the pictures with them on it are the prime ones being sought."

"What should we do with them?"

"That's a tough call." Vince rubbed his chin. "Even if we knew who the culprit was, handing them over to him could get us killed. Burning them is also out of the question. The killer won't believe that. Turning them over to the police could be dangerous. Lorenzo has a few cops in his pocket. I have a good friend in the FBI, but if we managed to get rid of them anonymously, we might never learn the identity of J.D., and that wouldn't stop J.D. or Kirby going after you. You could run. What's most important to you, Mia—finding your brother's killer or your safety?"

"You already know the answer to that. You'll put your life on the line to find Ethan's killer. I'll do no less to find Andy's. In his note, he said I had to kill them or run. I intend to do the former."

"Have you ever killed a person?"

"No, but I have a job to do, and like all the jobs I did with Andy, it'll be handled expertly." Mia's eyes darkened with rage.

"I don't doubt that for a minute. Now we just have to figure out who the target is."

"Give me Kirby's address. I'll disguise my appearance, make a house call, and tell him who I am.

If he's the guy responsible for Andy's death and behind the hunt for the photos, I doubt he's a big enough idiot to shoot me before he gets the location of the photos."

"I don't want you to go to see him," he said firmly.

Mia felt he was ordering her to stay away from Kirby, which she intended to ignore, but she needed the address. "If you are so opposed to that idea, lay out a better plan."

"You could go to work with a bug attached to your purse. Whoever wants these photos is actively seeking them. Someone will be making a move toward you soon."

Mia nodded in agreement. Suddenly, Gunther popped into her head. "Oh, Hank Gunther invited me to go with him to a banquet Thursday night. He seems overly interested in me. He wanted me to be part of the presentation team. What do you think? Any possibility he could be J.D.?"

"I imagine a lot of guys are overly interested in you. The banquet is tomorrow night?"

Mia nodded.

"That's short notice."

"He said he planned to invite me earlier, but there was a chance he wouldn't be able to attend. That's probably because he had some money problems— Lorraine told me about it on the way to the fundraiser. Gunther was on the verge of losing his Mercedes dealership to a partner he had borrowed money from. He had Lewis change a presentation from Mercedes to BMW, which would make sense under those circumstances. Then something changed, and he wanted a presentation for both Mercedes and BMW. His financial woes must have vanished. It could be completely legit—a new partner?"

"Just because his financial situation changed doesn't mean he played a role in anything devious."

"He gives me strange vibes. Unless a potential other lead surfaces, I'm going to accept his invitation."

"Where's the banquet going to be held?"

"He never said, but it's called the 'Business Owners of the Year Awards Banquet.' He's getting an award."

Vince tapped on the computer. "That banquet is real. Tomorrow night. Hank Gunther is listed as an honoree."

"I told him I'd call him today and let him know if I could make it." Mia pulled out her cell phone and then rummaged through her purse for Gunther's card. She turned it over to his handwritten cell number, punched in a few of the digits, and suddenly stopped. Mia stared at the number, trying to recall where she had seen it.

"What's wrong?"

"Gunther's private cell number seems familiar. I can't place it."

"Let me see the card."

Mia handed it over.

"Mia, your intuition is right on the mark. This is the number associated with 'No Caller ID.' The text message you received at the fundraiser was sent from Hank Gunther's phone."

She tilted her head. "Hank Gunther? But he was at the fundraiser and wanted me to have a drink with him after."

"Maybe someone else used his phone to send the text."

Any hesitation she had about going out with Gunther was gone. "Gunther might not be J.D., but he either knows him or Kirby. Something I intend to find out tomorrow night."

Vince tapped on his computer. "There are a few tickets left to the banquet. I'm ordering one." He continued tapping. "There. Done."

Mia placed the call to Gunther. After he answered and they greeted each other, she said, "I've been able to get out of my prior engagement, so I can go with you to the banquet."

"Wonderful. I'll pick you up at 6:30."

"See you then." She disconnected. "I'll be going to my apartment tomorrow after work."

"I don't want you to be there alone. Call me when you're heading there, and I'll meet you in the lobby."

Without voicing any objection, Mia gathered the pictures and put them back in the metal box.

"Do you want to put the box in the safe?"

"No." Mia smiled. "If someone breaks into your house, searching for the photos, the safe is the first place they'd look."

"You don't think this house is secure?"

"No place is completely secure. And if someone connected to the Russo family is after them, you don't have enough guards to hold off an onslaught of thugs."

"Good point. But with the security systems, it wouldn't take long for reinforcements to arrive." He glanced at his watch. "It's almost time for us to be heading to the police station."

"I want to change." Carrying her purse and the metal box, she hurried upstairs to the guest bedroom. Mia only took a few things out of her suitcase since she doubted she'd be sleeping in that room.

Chapter 18

When Mia and Vince reached the police station, Vince took a seat in the lobby and Lieutenant Collins escorted her to an interview room.

"This won't take long," Lieutenant Collins said. "Do you mind if I record this interview?"

"No."

The lieutenant flipped on a switch. "Please state your name for the record." After Mia did that, he asked, "How many times were you at the LeMonte house prior to Monday evening?"

"Twice. Last Wednesday evening and Sunday night."

"On those two occasions, besides the chef and a maid, did you see anyone else in the house?"

"No."

"Anyone in the yard?"

"I did see a uniformed guard outside the house."

"Before being driven through the gate, did you observe any cars parked along the street?"

Mia shook her head. "No, but I can't say for sure

there weren't any cars."

Lieutenant Collins rose. "That will be all for now. I'll contact you if we have any other questions."

The Lieutenant walked her to the lobby. "Thank you for coming in, Miss Sloan." He shook her hand.

"That was quick," Vince said as they walked to the car.

"Just the way I wanted it to be."

On the way back to the house, Vince said, "An insurance agent is coming to the house to discuss the theft with Oliver. I thought we'd eat now and avoid being there. Would you prefer to go to a restaurant or grab a quick bite at a diner?"

"Diner. Oliver's filing an insurance claim for the diamonds?"

"Yes. That's the customary thing to do after a robbery. If the man behind Andy's death believes you have the uncut diamonds and the pictures, that could give you some leverage."

"I see your point. I might need that pretense to stay alive."

Shortly before ten, Vince and Mia returned to his place. She had expected to meet Oliver, but the house was quiet. It appeared Oliver and the staff had already retired for the evening.

Vince escorted her upstairs and guided her into his room.

Mia saw her suitcase and belongings in there. "Does this mean you intend for me to stay with you?"

He gave her a sensuous smile and began unbuttoning her blouse. "That's the plan."

As her blouse fell from her shoulders, Vince held her tightly and slightly raised her off the floor. He brushed her hair to one side, and planted kisses up her neck. His touch was soft and passionate.

She flushed with pleasure as her body tingled. The warmth of his breath sent chills through her as he explored her mouth with his tongue. Mia gasped when his fingers trailed up her thigh. With all her doubts about Vince resolved, Mia let herself get lost in his arms.

After spending the night enjoying every move Vince made, Mia went downstairs to have breakfast with a smile on her face. The table had only been set for two. "Won't Oliver be joining us?"

"No." Vince pulled out a chair for her. "He left early for the jewelry store. Oliver wanted to get some work done before customers arrived. May I drive you to work today?"

Mia shook her head. "Since I've always taken a cab or the subway to work and I'm going out with Gunther, I don't want rumors spreading that I have a boyfriend."

He reached across the table and took her hand. "Mia, that's a label I want."

"That's a label you've got, but let's keep it between you and me."

He smiled. "Agreed."

* * *

When Mia arrived at work, Lorraine rushed toward her. "You won't believe this," Lorraine said, her face glowing and her eyes shimmering. "Oliver LeMonte is going with me to my neighbor's party. He's so dreamy. Isn't that cool?"

"But you said you were going to invite Vince to that party."

"I called him. His cousin, Oliver, is a little depressed. I sure can see why. He had a whole bunch of diamonds stolen. Poor guy. Vince thought I was the perfect person to cheer Oliver up, and Oliver had already mentioned to Vince that he wanted to go out with me. Oliver called me last night to ask what the attire is for the engagement. *Attire.* He is so formal, not like me. I hope I don't blow it."

"All you need to do is be yourself. I heard his ex-wife was rather stuffy, so you'll be a ray of sunshine."

"You think so?"

"Absolutely."

As soon as Mia stepped into her office, she retrieved the ring from the book, slipped it on her finger and marched into Lewis's office without knocking.

Lewis's eyes shot to her.

Before he had a chance to say anything, Mia dropped the receipt on his desk. "Next time you start making wild accusations about me, you better check your facts. Lewis, we've worked together for six years, and you actually believed I was a thief. You have no idea how bad that made me feel. It's going to take a long time for me to get over it."

Lewis looked at the receipt. "Mia, I'm sorry. I didn't call LeMonte's to see if you stole it. I only called to help you."

Mia grabbed the receipt out of his hand. "I'm sorry too, Lewis. Sorry that you needed proof before you'd believe me." She turned on her heel and went back to her office.

Mia forced herself to stay focused on her work and not think about the pictures or her date with Gunther. But the closer it got to quitting time, her resolve began to waver, and she found her head bobbing between the documents on her desk and the clock on the wall.

At 4:50 p.m., she gave up, cleared off her desk, and called Vince to tell him she was leaving work.

Like it had become her habit, Mia kept checking the cab's mirrors for a tail as she rode to her apartment. Not spotting any cars following her, she still sensed that she was being followed. *Has a more professional group been hired for the job?*

Getting out of the cab, she scanned the cars parked along the street. Vince's car wasn't among them. As Mia walked into the lobby, Vince stepped out of the parking garage elevator. She took his hand and pulled him out of earshot from the concierge. "How did you get in the parking garage?"

He caressed her cheek. "Your parking garage isn't very secure. I just followed a car in."

"Did you see any shady characters?"

"Possibly. On parking level two, I noticed three men climbing into a SUV. One looked like a guy who followed you in a BMW a couple of days ago."

"You think they might've paid my apartment a visit?"

"Maybe. You'll have to determine if anything looks out of place."

Reaching her apartment, Mia unlocked the door and held her breath, fearing the worst. As she pushed it open, she exhaled. Nothing looked disturbed, but when she stepped over the threshold, she noticed her furniture had been slightly moved.

"See anything out of place?" Vince followed her inside.

"Someone has been here." She headed straight to

the coffee maker and turned it over. Scratch marks were in the plastic surface surrounding the screws. She cringed, knowing that hiding spot had not been as secure as she had thought. Vince had been right— the thugs would've found the pictures. They wouldn't have been safe anywhere in her apartment.

Vince wrapped his arms around her. "When we've taken care of whoever is behind the search for the pictures, I need to return to Paris. I have anxious clients waiting for me. I don't want to leave you." He smothered her lips with his. "Would you consider going with me?"

"Vince, I have a job here."

"Quit, and come work with me."

"Doing what?"

"Investigating crimes. You can use all your acquired special skills, but with me, you'll be on the right side of the law."

"But I…"

"Mia, will you really be happy just working for an ad agency? Won't you miss the excitement and danger, that adrenaline rush your night job gave you?"

I felt that adrenaline high escaping from Andy's shop. She doubted she'd be content going to the office every day and living a normal life. She'd never lived a normal life since she had started working for her father. Even when she occasionally dreaded meeting Andy, knowing there was another job on the horizon, another possibility they'd get caught, it always stirred a sense of excitement. She never would've turned down any of those jobs, and sometimes she felt restless waiting for the next one. Anticipation surged through her, thinking of working with Vince.

"I might. Until we know the identity of Andy's

killer, I just can't think about anything else."

Vince held her tighter. "Mia, I want you in my life. I'll always want you in my life."

Mia also wanted Vince. Besides her brother, he was the first man she had loved, but she feared telling him would make her too vulnerable. "Gunther will be here in half an hour. I need to get ready." She gathered a few things and headed into the bathroom.

When the concierge called Mia's unit to let her know Gunther was in the lobby, she said she'd be down soon. She flipped off the intercom and turned to Vince. "He's almost ten minutes early."

"He must be anxious." Vince zipped up her dress, kissed her neck, and ran his hands down her body.

"I don't have time for that." Mia winked and broke away to finish putting on her makeup.

Five minutes later, she slipped on the jacket that went with her dress, kissed Vince goodbye, and left. She dreaded having to pretend she was interested in Gunther in order to get information from him. Knowing Vince would be close by made it tolerable.

Gunther escorted Mia to a Mercedes in front of the building. Driving to the hotel where the banquet was to be held, Gunther kept looking around like he was searching for a tail. Mia wondered if some of his men had spotted someone else following her.

Stopping in front of a gated side entrance to the parking garage, the one for employees, Gunther pulled out a card and held it in front of the scanner.

Mia guessed that award winners were afforded special amenities by the organization, and being guaranteed a close parking spot was probably one of those. But instead of parking near the door, Gunther passed numerous empty stalls and drove to the end of the row and parked next to a limo.

Like a gentlemen, he looped around the car and opened the door for Mia.

The minute she climbed out, the limo door flew open, and an armed man stepped out.

Chapter 19

Nigel Dawson, Feinstein's oft-absent partner, slid to the door. "Thank you, Hank."

"We're square?" Gunther asked.

"Yes. Go collect your *award*."

"What's this all about, Hank?" Mia positioned herself to fight her way out, but then two armed men came around the front of the limo. The odds were against her.

Gunther briefly glanced at Mia, and without saying another word, strode away.

"Get her purse," Dawson ordered. "And check her."

The closest armed man grabbed her purse and stuck it into a black BMW across from the limo. Another thug ran a wand over her. Mia knew he was looking for bugs. Her eyes swept around, searching for other people on that parking level. Not seeing anyone, she stood stoically, refusing to let the man in the limo rattle her.

"Clear." The wand-yielding thug put the gadget

away.

"Mr. Dawson, what is it that you want?" Mia asked, sounding irritated.

"Please call me J.D., and I'd appreciate you accompanying me to the factory."

"Factory?"

"Just get in the car, Mia."

Assuming she couldn't escape without being shot, Mia climbed into the limo. An armed man got in after her.

With the limo's heavily tinted windows, no one could see her inside.

Mia eyed the interior, looking for something she might be able to use as a weapon. Two bottles, one wine and one whisky, and glasses along with a corkscrew were on a tray attached to the car frame near the door. Mia intended to snatch the corkscrew when she exited the limo.

As the limo drove along a highway, Mia's thoughts turned to Vince. *How will he react when he sees I'm not with Gunther?* She guessed it wouldn't be a pleasant scene.

Mia turned to Dawson, who was busy tapping on his phone. "J.D., what's this all about?"

"I'll explain everything when we reach our destination."

Mia looked out the window and noticed the limo was entering a freeway. Wondering how far away the factory was, Mia's eyes moved back to J.D., and gazing at his profile, she suddenly suspected that J.D. was the man in the picture who held a weapon over Luca Russo. He was older, but the nose, deep-set eyes, and high forehead were the same.

While J.D. continued tapping on his cell phone, it

rang. He stopped tapping and answered it. "Yeah, I've got her...but we still have twenty miles to go.....Got it." He clicked off. "Take the next exit."

Mia forced herself to remain calm. *This change of plans probably isn't good.*

The limo turned off the freeway, drove for a few minutes, and then pulled over to the side of the road. The door opened. A heavily-armed, freakishly tall man stood outside.

The man bent down and peered into the limo. "The boss wants to take her," he said in a firm, steely voice.

J.D. looked at Mia. "Get out." His sneer made her skin crawl.

Mia stumbled toward the door, bumping into the tray on her way. The bottles rattled but remained on the tray. Gripping the corkscrew, she pushed it up her sleeve, and climbed out of the vehicle.

The tall man led her to a limo parked behind J.D.'s and opened the door.

Mia noticed a black SUV behind that limo, and wondered how many men had been tasked with extracting information from her. She was directed to sit on the same seat as the man inside. *Lorenzo Russo.* With the exception of his graying hair, there was no mistaking him as the man in the picture with her mother.

He held out his hand. "Mia, before we leave, would you mind giving me the corkscrew you so cleverly took from J.D.'s limo?"

Mia wanted to shout, "Yes, I mind giving it up." But she removed the corkscrew from her sleeve and handed it to Russo.

He gave it to the freakishly tall man. "Return this

to J.D., and tell him he should be more observant next time. On second thought, no need to tell him anything. Shut the door. You'll be riding up front."

After everything Mia had heard about the Russos, she would've expected to be horrified being in the company of one of them. Her mother was always kind and loving to everyone. *What had she seen in this man who committed heinous crimes?*

Russo's eyes fixed on Mia, and then he reached over and touched her cheek.

Mia flinched.

"Mia, I'm not going to harm you, and I won't allow anyone else to harm you."

What does that mean? No torture? Maybe he intends to use truth serum to find where I put the photos.

"I didn't want you in J.D.'s limo any longer than necessary. I don't trust him anymore. Not that I ever really did, but he was tolerable."

Mia felt the intensity of his gaze.

"You look like your mother. You don't have brown eyes or dark hair, but it's easy to see you're her daughter. I loved your mother very much." A sad expression flashed on his face, and Mia suddenly felt sorry for the crime boss. "I guess I still do. I wanted to marry her, but she wanted her children to have a normal childhood, something that would've been impossible living with me. We agreed that she'd live at Thelma's farm with you and Andy, and I'd never go there. In exchange, she'd come and see me whenever she could, which wasn't as often as I would've liked. She'd always showed me pictures of you along with some videos of you and Andy playing, but your mother always took them back to the farm with her.

"Mia, I'm so sorry about what happened to Andy.

I didn't get wind that J.D. was in pursuit of those photos, the ones you began researching at the library, until it was too late for Andy."

How did he know what I was doing at the library?

Russo went on. "J.D. believes there are two sets of those photos, and one is in my possession. Otherwise, he wouldn't have contacted me." Russo patted Mia's knee. "Even though Andy didn't know me, I liked him. He protected you. When his body is released, I will make arrangements to have him buried by your mother and Thelma."

Mia's eyes misted. Andy's death still tore at her heart. Russo wrapped his arms around her. "My little Valentine, his death will be avenged. You'll never see Nigel James Dawson again, nor will anyone else."

Mia was born on Valentine's Day. "My little Valentine" was a name her mother called her whenever she got hurt or something upset her.

Russo went on. "I would've handled J.D. earlier, but first I wanted to know what, if anything, he knew about you. Now it's clear he believes you're Leo Carlyle's child."

What is Lorenzo Russo saying? Is he my dad? Mia recalled all the flowers that were delivered to her mother when she was dying. Tons and tons of flowers. And at the gravesite, a man stood on the hill. She thought he was Leo Carlyle, but now she realized it was the man holding her.

Russo released her. "Mia, it's dangerous for you to have the pictures that J.D. sought. I should've had someone retrieve them years ago, but I had promised your mother never to go to the farm. She feared if I ever went there, I'd contaminate it, and it would no longer be a safe place." A faint smile crossed his lips.

"She was probably right. My moves are often followed. Will you give me the pictures?"

Mia had so many questions streaming through her head. "Why did you keep the pictures in the first place?"

"J.D. claimed he also had someone take pictures, and on one of them, I'm leaning over my brother's body and your mother is in the background. At that time, J.D. and my father were friends. J.D. threatened he would hand over all of his pictures if I exposed him as my brother's killer. Since I was there, but in the building's lounge when it went down, I couldn't prove I had nothing to do with it, and I didn't want your mother being dragged into the mess. I kept the pictures to show that J.D. was the shooter in case the pictures he claimed he had ever surfaced.

"I wanted a picture with your mother and me on it. Had it not been for that, none of the pictures you saw would've ever been taken. The photographer is a loyal employee. After your mother and I left him, he heard shooting and checked it out. It's fortunate he took pictures because I believe it was J.D.'s goal to pin my brother's killing on me."

"Why would he do that?"

"We had a disagreement over a matter which cost him an appreciable amount of money. He never did get along with my brother." Russo stroked her arm. "Can't get over how much you look like your mother. Mia, will you give me those pictures?"

"Yes." All of her defenses were down. *I believe him.*

"Bring them with you to work tomorrow. I'll have a courier pick them up. He'll claim he's there to pick up something for Mr. Dawson." He pulled a ring out of his pocket. "I want you to wear this. It'll keep you safe from criminals in our *little* town." He smiled.

Mia studied the inch wide gold engraved band. Her mother wore one just like it, and it was the only piece of jewelry she wanted to be buried with. Since the ring reminded Mia of a wedding band and her mother had worn it on her left hand, Mia moved the LeMonte ring to her left hand and slipped the band on her right ring finger.

"How did you know my size?"

"Good guess. I would like you to make me a promise."

"What?" Mia felt apprehensive.

"That you'll never tell anyone you're my daughter. That information in the wrong hands could become a dangerous problem."

Mia's mother had kept the identity of her biological father well-hidden, and Mia intended to do no less. She was still having a hard time grasping that she was his child, the child of a man feared by many. "I'll keep that secret. I won't tell anyone we're related."

Russo took Mia's hand and gazed at her. "Would you mind if I dropped into your life from time to time."

"You'll always be welcome to visit me, but I might be leaving the country."

"Going to Paris with Vince Tolbert?"

She tilted her head and smiled. "Thinking about it."

"You should go. And remember your promise— absolutely no one should know I'm your father. Tell Vince I had a beef with J.D. Besides killing Andy, J.D. also killed Vince's cousin, Ethan." Russo pulled a folded business card out of his pocket. "If you are ever in trouble or need anything, call this number."

Mia looked at the handwritten number on the card.

"Memorize it, or put it in a very secure location. If you should call, say you are M.C."

Mia nodded.

"Your boyfriend is probably panicking. I'm going to drop you off at a diner so you can call him. Your purse will be there." Russo slid open the panel that separated the front seat from the passengers. "Go to the Towne Diner."

Five minutes later, the limo arrived.

Russo hugged Mia and kissed her forehead. "I'm glad we finally had a chance to meet."

"So am I."

The car door opened, and Mia slipped out.

When she stepped into the diner, a bearded, elderly man handed Mia her purse, and then he walked out the door. Mia sat down in a booth and placed a call to Vince.

Chapter 20

While Mia drank a cup of coffee, she deleted the pictures on her cell that had cost Andy's life, except for the one of her mother and Lorenzo Russo. She found herself mesmerized by it as she replayed everything he had told her. Mia's mother had kept his existence a secret to protect her. Growing up, Andy and she had often speculated about their father, thinking he was a spy or something like that since they never saw him, but their mother never divorced him. And they both thought when their mom took off on "farm co-op trips," it was to see him. *We weren't one-hundred percent wrong, but it was to see my father, a father Andy and I didn't share.*

"Mia," Vince said, snapping her back to the present. He pulled her out of her seat and enveloped her in his arms. "I thought I had lost you forever." They slid into the booth. "It never entered my mind that Gunther would hand you over to J.D. in the parking garage. Once he drove through the employee gate, Owen went and parked on another level....What happened? How did you get away?"

"I didn't have to escape. I was dropped off here."

Vince's eyes narrowed and he put his hand on top of Mia's. "Did you just tell him where the pictures were, and he let you go?"

"No. That wasn't how it went." She noticed his scraped and bruised knuckles. "What happened to your hand?"

"I needed information. After I finished with Gunther, he was in no condition to accept his award. What happened?"

Mia scanned the diner. "This might not be a good place to talk. I'll fill you in at your house." She took a sip of coffee.

As she put down the cup, Vince stared at her fingers. Pointing to the ring she had just received, he asked, "Where did you get that?"

She whispered, "Lorenzo Russo gave it to me."

His eyes met hers. "We need to talk. Are you ready to go?"

"Yes."

Driving toward his house, Mia contemplated how much to tell Vince about the conversation with Lorenzo Russo. Her mother had felt she'd be safer not being part of the Russo family, and her father agreed. She intended to keep that secret and fill in gaps in her story with lies.

Vince occasionally glanced at her without saying anything.

Mia wondered what was going through his mind as they drove in silence. "Will Oliver still be awake when we get there?"

"I'm sure he'll be in bed."

When they entered the house, Vince led her

straight to his bedroom and closed the door. "Mia, LeMonte makes those rings for the Russo family. I know what they mean. Why did Lorenzo Russo give you one?"

"Let me explain everything."

"Okay, explain." Vince took her hand, and they sat down on the bed.

Mia told him everything that happened from when Gunther pulled into the parking lot to her climbing into Russo's limo and then said, "As you know from the picture, Lorenzo Russo and my mother fell in love. He wanted her to marry him, but Mom didn't want Andy and me around criminals—funny how that turned out. He knew we were her kids, but he never met us.

"J.D. killed Luca," Mia began and relayed everything Lorenzo Russo had told her about the events of that night and the pictures. "When J.D. called Russo to help find that set of pictures, it was after J.D. had killed Andy." Mia swallowed hard and her eyes filled with tears.

Vince put his arm around her shoulders.

In a strained voice, Mia continued. "Russo will handle Andy's burial when his body is released. He knows where my mom is buried, and he'll bury Andy near her. So you don't need to worry about dealing with that."

"Mia, it wouldn't have been a problem for me to take care of that."

"I know, but Russo wants to do it. Maybe he feels a little responsible for Andy's death. Had those pictures not been buried at Aunt Thelma's, Andy would still be alive."

Mia brushed a few tears off her cheek.

Vince hugged her. "Maybe we should wait and talk about your ordeal tomorrow."

"No. I want to finish. Russo asked me for the pictures. He promised I wouldn't be harmed if I gave them to him, and I believe him. I'm planning to hand them over tomorrow."

"And what about the ring he gave you?"

Mia held up her hand. "He said this ring will keep me safe in his town."

"Mia, those rings are reserved for family members."

"I guess he's made some exceptions. My mom was buried wearing a ring just like this. He felt bad about Andy. He probably didn't want me to end up the same way. And he confirmed J.D. also killed Ethan. He's going to take care of J.D. No details. But he said I'd never see Nigel James Dawson again and neither would anyone else."

"So now we can move on." Vince kissed Mia and held her tight against his chest. "I went crazy when you didn't show up at the banquet. I can't stand the thought of losing you again. I've never before cared about anyone the way I do you. Will you marry me?"

"Vince, we haven't known each other that long. It's a little early to be talking about getting married."

"I love you, Mia. That's all that matters. Will you be my wife?"

After losing Andy, her mom, Aunt Thelma, and the man she thought was her father, Mia knew how short life could be. She gazed into Vince's eyes. *I believe he loves me.* Mia had always feared falling in love because of her criminal activities, but Vince knew about that and he still wanted her. "Only if I can be your partner in the investigation racket."

"Racket? It's legit."

"You're right about the adrenalin high. I don't want to give up the possibility of never getting it again."

* * *

Mia had sublet her apartment to Lorraine and two weeks later packed the last box to be taken with her and Vince to Paris. A moving team stacked her final boxes onto a dolly, and Vince added two suitcases to their load.

"That's everything." He put his arm around Mia's waist. "Do you want to have lunch on the way to the airport or eat on the plane?"

"I've never been on a private plane before. Let's eat there."

Vince whispered in her ear. "And then we can enjoy the bedroom after lunch, my soon-to-be wife."

Mia smiled at him. "That will make the whole trip worthwhile, my soon-to-be husband."

Are you ready to go?"

"I want to look around a little longer."

"I have a few things in my car I want them to take. I'll follow them down and meet you in the lobby."

After the door closed behind them, Mia wandered through her apartment, making sure she hadn't left anything behind. In the bedroom, she picked up her purse and grabbed the handle of her small travel suitcase that she intended to take into the plane's cabin.

She went into the kitchen and looked into each cabinet. Mia was leaving all the dishes, pots and pans, and silverware for Lorraine. She turned around without looking and knocked Vince's briefcase on the floor. *He forgot this! It's good I did a final check.* Mia saw the lock had snapped open when it tumbled to the floor. Gathering up the contents, Mia noticed a black velvet pouch tucked into the bottom of the briefcase. She pulled it out and loosened the tie. Mia gazed at the uncut diamonds inside. She smiled to herself as she closed up the bag and put it back into the briefcase along with all of the spilled items. *Oliver filed an insurance claim. His family will collect the full value of the stones. I guess Vince doesn't always operate on the right side of the law after all. That makes me love him even more.*

Mia threw the strap of Vince's briefcase over her shoulder, picked up her purse, rolled her suitcase out of the apartment, and headed to a new life with the man she loved.

About the Author

Inge-Lise Goss, a USA Today and Multi-Award Winning Best Selling author, was born in Denmark, raised in Utah, and now lives in the foothills of Red Rock Canyon with her husband and their dog, Ted. She spends most of her time in her den writing stories. There, with her muse by her side, her imagination has no boundaries, and her dreams come alive. When she's not pounding away on the keyboard, she can be found reading, rowing, or trying to perfect her golf game, which she fears is a lost cause.

www.Inge-LiseGoss.com

Note from the Author

Thank you readers! I feel humbled and honored that you took time to read this story. If you enjoyed it, please consider posting a review on Amazon. All reviews—positive or negative— are greatly appreciated!

Best wishes,
Inge-Lise

Other Books By Inge-Lise Goss

Compelled

No Freedom: An A.I. Thriller

Gwynn Reznick Mystery Series

The Cost of Crude – Book 1

Cisco Bandits Crude – Book 2

The Tegen Series

The Tegen Cave – Book 1

Tegen Justice – Book 2

Tegen Punishment – Book 3